You read

Significant Australians

reflect on their teenage reading

David Thomson

Connor Court Publishing

You Read What?
David Thomson
Published in 2024 by Connor Court Publishing Pty Ltd

Connor Court Publishing Pty Ltd
PO Box 7257
Redland Bay QLD 4165
sales@connorcourt.com
www.connorcourt.com

Printed in Australia

ISBN: 9781922815989

By the same author

But Memories Remain (co-editor)

The Loneliest Boy in New York (poems)

Stanley Wynton Kurrle

Risk a Smile (poems)

The Old School: A Portrait of Caulfield Grammar School in 50 Lives

A Goodly Heritage Series 2 (editor)

In memory of my dear mother

Aggie Isabel (Jane) Thomson

1906 – 2011

who taught me about books

Introduction

When I returned to my old school to teach English and Legal Studies, I asked my Year 11 English class to tell me what books they were reading for pleasure. I was not surprised to learn that some said they weren't reading any books other than those set for study. Most, however, were reading books occasionally but only a few were regular readers.

After some discussion, I asked them how they find out what is worth reading. Their responses were fairly predictable: "I saw it in a shop", "Ask Mum or Dad", "My mate read it and said it was okay", even "I'd ask a teacher". Most were not habitués of the local library. I asked them whose opinion they would value in regard to books that were worth reading. After some more discussion, their answers boiled down to one: "It would be good to ask people who have been successful if they were readers and what books they read when they were our age". A class project was born!

A model letter was drafted, the library copy of "Who's Who in Australia" took a bit of a battering and students came up with a list of names. They sent letters to about 250 people, with replies to come to me.

My Year 11 classmates have devised a project, the aim of which is to increase and widen the reading habits of boys at our school.

In the belief that your response will help stimulate worthwhile reading, the following question is put to you: "Which book or books were your favourites or influenced you most as a teenager and why?"

We plan to display responses and will publish a selection of the replies we receive.

Please do not feel that a long essay is required; a few lines would be quite acceptable.

Over 130 replies were received and, together with a brief biography of each writer, make up this book. Was the project a success? The librarian told me that many of my class asked for books which were recommended. We had a lot of fun with the project and I hope the long-term effect was a positive one. Many members of that class have become significant Australians themselves.

Aside from providing my students with suggestions for their own reading, I thought there may have been common threads which would run through the responses. I was wrong. A huge number of books and writers were mentioned. Shakespeare's plays were listed by 18 respondents; books by Charles Dickens by 19; Kipling by 12; and the Bible by 11. Only Jim Cairns, Sir Zelman Cowen, Bob Hawke, Sir Laurence Hartnett, Barry Jones, Sir William McKell, Louis Kahan, Clifford Last , Andrew Peacock John Béchervaise, Clive Caldwell, Sir Robert Jackson and Sir Frank Little read books as teenagers which linked in some way to their future careers and a mere handful read books by Australian authors. There was not a lot of difference between the reading habits of male and female respondents.

Just for the record, the books which I read as a teenager and thoroughly enjoyed were *For the White Cockade* by Admiral Lord Mountevans, *Chang* by Elizabeth Morse, *Lord of the Flies* by William Golding, *Her Privates We* by Frederic Manning, *Devil Water* by Anya Seton, *The Last Enemy* by Richard Hillary, *Ring of Bright Water* by Gavin Maxwell, *Death in Venice* by Thomas Mann and *Seven Pillars of Wisdom* by T.E. Lawrence. I also carried a small book of the poems of Keats in my blazer pocket.

Perhaps an English teacher might like to replicate my students' survey to see what the responses would be today. I think the picture might be very different.

The spelling and punctuation of the letters has been retained.

Contributors

Charles Abbott   15

Phillip Adams   17

Patsy Adam-Smith   18

Claudio Alcorso   21

Charles Anderson, VC   23

Bob Ansett   25

Sir Reginald Ansett   26

Doug Anthony   27

Julie Anthony   28

Sir Robert Askin   29

Sir Garfield Barwick   31

Marjorie Barnard   32

John Béchervaise   34

Sir Joh Bjelke-Petersen   36

Geoffrey Blainey   37

John Blight   39

Sir Henry Bolte   41

Sir Jack Brabham   42

John Brack   43

Russell Braddon   45

Sir Donald Bradman   46

John Bray   47

Niall Brennan   49

Sir Macfarlane Burnet   51

Jim Cairns   52

Clive Caldwell   53

Dame Carmen Callil   55

Sir Roderick Carnegie   57

Matt Carroll   59

Maie Casey   60

Nancy Cato	61
Don Charlwood	63
Manning Clark	65
Sir Rupert Clarke	67
Jon Cleary	69
H.C. "Nugget" Coombs	71
Sir Zelman Cowen	74
Finlay Crisp	76
Paul Cronin	79
Dymphna Cusack	80
John Beede Cusack	82
Sir James Darling	83
Sir Rohan Delacombe	85
Viscount De Lisle, VC	87
Stuart Devlin	88
Brian Dixon	89
Rosemary Dobson	90
Sir Edward "Weary" Dunlop	92
Dame Mary Durack	94
Geoffrey Dutton	96
Hughie Edwards, VC	98
Tony Eggleton	100
Herb Elliott	102
Sumner Locke Elliott	104
Noel Ferrier	106
Joan Fitzhardinge	108
Malcolm Fraser	110
Frank Galbally	112
Ken Hall	114
Rodney Hall	119
Dame Joan Hammond	121
Lang Hancock	124
Sir Keith Hancock	126

Pro Hart	127
Sir Laurence Hartnett	128
Sir Paul Hasluck	130
Stanley Hawes	132
Bob Hawke	135
Bishop John Hazlewood	137
Sir Robert Helpmann	139
Angas Holmes	141
A.D. Hope	143
Peter Howson	145
Barry Humphries	147
Robert Ingpen	149
Peter Isaacson	151
Kenneth Jack	152
Sir Robert Jackson	154
Sir Asher Joel	156
Ian Johnson	158
Barry Jones	160
Marilyn Jones	161
Louis Kahan	163
Peter Karmel	165
Nancy Keesing	167
Michael Kirby	170
Sir Richard Kirby	172
Leonie Kramer	174
Stanley Kurrle	176
John La Nauze	178
Don Lane	180
Clifford Last	181
Sir Condor Laucke	183
Phillip Law	185
Ray Lawler	187
Joan Lindsay	189

Archbishop Sir Frank Little	191
John McCallum	194
Alan McCulloch	196
F. Margaret McGuire	198
Sir William McKell	201
Sir Charles Mackerras	203
Ian McLaren	204
Sir William McMahon	208
Leonard Mann	209
Alan Marshall	210
Bert Newton	212
Gerald O'Collins	214
Andrew Peacock	215
Stuart Sayers	216
Sir Billy Snedden	218
Peter Sculthorpe	220
Dame Joan Sutherland	222
Colin Thiele	223
Lindsay Thompson	226
Archbishop Sir Frank Woods	227
Sir John Young	229
Bibliography of works cited	231
Acknowledgements	240

Charles Abbott

Born 1939

Charles Percy Abbott was born in Berrigan, New South Wales, and educated at Caulfield Grammar School and the University of Melbourne where he graduated in law. He played football with the University Blues and then with Hawthorn Football Club where he was a member of the 1961 Premiership Team. He joined the firm of Blake and Riggall (now Ashurst) and practised in London with Allen and Overy and in New York with White and Case. Growing up with horses, he started playing polo which took him all over the world. His racehorse, Gurner's Lane, won the Melbourne Cup in 1982. In 1985, he brought Prince Charles to Melbourne to play polo at Werribee Park.

When I was at Caulfield Grammar, I went to hospital for a few days with a displaced nose from a football clash. I took with me a novel *Gone with the Wind* by the American writer Margaret Mitchell, who had won the Pulitzer Prize for Fiction in 1937. I got to the part where Rhett Butler was in Georgia and he rode down the streets, smiling, tipping his hat, the small bundle that was Bonnie perched before him on the saddle. Everyone smiled back, spoke with enthusiasm and looked with affection on the little girl, whereas, her mother, Scarlett, was not so sure. One day, Bonnie was riding her pony, Mr Butler, and approaching a jump. Scarlett called out: *"No! No! Oh, Bonnie stop!"*

Even as she leaned from the window there was a fearful sound of splintering wood, a hoarse cry from Rhett, a melee of blue velvet and flying hooves on the ground. Then Mr Butler scrambled to his feet and trotted off with an empty saddle.

15

After Bonnie's death, the story is very sad.

Having read *Gone with the Wind*, I realised that the refusal of my parents to give me a pony at an early stage was sensible. It did not, however, stop my love of galloping horses on the Riverina plains or playing polo, galloping at 40 miles an hour, with dangerous clashes and falls under and over ponies and players. The excitement was great when travelling abroad when we were lent ponies from the stables of our hosts and hostesses.

My mother and father were brought up under strict colonial English traditions. One of these was to have a correct understanding of English and history. As a result, my father gave me his 12 volumes of Charles Dickens, which he told me he had read by the time he was 12- years-old. I had difficulty abiding by these rules but I ploughed on reading. By the time I had read five Charles Dickens novels: *A Christmas Carol, Great Expectations, Oliver Twist, Bleak House* and *Tale of Two Cities*. I was in New York in 1966 reading *The Great Gatsby, To Kill a Mockingbird* and *Lord of the Flies* and I had already read *1984*. I had kept the Dickens volumes and they are still in a butterfly wood bookcase which I bought from Blake & Riggall at my first meeting as a Partner. The firm was moving from 120 William Street to the BHP building at the corner of William and Bourke Streets in 1991.

Without doubt, Dad could see I was enthralled with horses and, to avoid the comics, he gave my brother Bill and me the English novel *The Black Riders* by Amy Violet Needham, the daughter of Colonel Charles Needham, of the 1st Life Guards of the British Army, the King's bodyguard. She wrote the book in 1939, the year I was born. The book was riveting, set in a mystic empire with cavalry officers and Count Jasper the Terrible as a member of the Parliament. The story is of an orphan boy, Dick Fauconbois, who becomes a member of a rebel movement led by a saint-like figure called Far Away Moses, the chief enemy of Count Jasper. With mystical characters and cavalry horses and all, Bill and I were mesmerized. I was only 10 years old.

Phillip Adams

Born 1939

Phillip Adams, AO, FAHA, FRSA Adams was born in Maryborough, Victoria. He left school before completing his secondary education and found work in advertising. He left the advertising industry in the 1980s for journalism. He wrote regular columns for "The Age" and a variety of Australian newspapers as well as contributions for "The New York Times", the "Financial Times" and "The Times" of London. He currently writes a weekly column for "The Australian". He played a key role in the revival of the Australian film industry during the 1970s. He was the author of a 1969 report which led to legislation by Prime Minister John Gorton in 1970 for an Australian Film and Television Development Corporation (later the Australian Film Commission) and the Experimental Film Fund. Together with Barry Jones, he was a motivating force behind the Australian Film Television and Radio School which was established under the Whitlam government.

I once answered your question at length in a newspaper column but I can remember neither the date nor the publication. For me, one book will suffice – *The Grapes of Wrath*. I remember having run out of Biggles, Billabong and William books at the local library and being handed Steinbeck's novel from the adults' section by a left-wing librarian. The story of dust bowl and depression had a profound influence, leading me to join the Communist Party at 16. These days, of course, I'm an enfeebled old conservative who dabbles with the ALP – but even that commitment dates from Steinbeck's revelations.

I find the book faintly embarrassing to read 27 years later – the prose is a little purple – but I am still haunted by its images and ideas.

Patsy Adam-Smith

1924 – 2001

*Patricia Adam-Smith, AO, OBE, was the author of
more than 30 publications on a wide range of topics.
She grew up in several Victoria country towns and
attended local schools. In World War II she was a
Voluntary Aid Detachment nurse and then a merchant
marine radio operator from 1954 to 1960. In 1970, she
became Manuscripts Field Officer for the State Library
of Victoria until 1982. She was a Director of the Royal
Humane Society and a committee member of the Museum
of Victoria. As a writer, she is probably best known for
her much-lauded 1978 book "The Anzacs" which was
made into a 13-part television series.*

There was only one book for me – literally one until I left home at
sixteen. But I was permitted to read this, although only this. That
odd state of affairs has nothing to do with your project and if it
did I would not speak of it. The omission of reading in my early
childhood led me to engulf and delight myself with books when
I did find them, in a way that no forced or structured reading
programme could have done. My catholic reading tastes I believe
came from discovering books for myself (when I just read the
Bible, aged seventeen, I went straight through it and when I'd
finished the New Testament I started again on the Old. I can still
hover for days on Hagar. What a woman! Wow.)

There was one thing that dismayed me about the *Bible*: I'd made
up my mind to write and suddenly I found that all the plots that
could possibly be used had been used already and with such style,
beauty and economy there would be no point in writing anything
ever again I thought.

The several bush schools I attended for the few years I was at school (I left for good at thirteen) were poor as were the times and had no library, indeed no books at all, no text books, but there were "Readers" which we could not take from the one-room school.

That one book. It was called *The Children's Treasure House* and was sold via a coupon in Melbourne's *Sun* newspaper in 1935 when I was 10 years old. It had 768 pages and was pure 24 carat gold. (I guess that in those mean days of the Great Depression whatever it cost must have seemed outrageous in our part of the bush.)

It was a "Treasure House". In it I met Anthony Trollope, Rose Macauley and Charles and Mary Lamb, Victor Hugo, Sir Henry Newbolt (Capten, art tha sleepin' there below?) and Shakespeare, Keats and G.K. Chesterton. There were stories from *The Mabinogion* and tales from the *Gesta Romanorum*. In it I met Ratty and Mole for the first time, Perseus and the Gorgon, Ulysses and Polyphemus. " . . . our echoes roll from soul to soul, and grow forever and forever" wrote Tennyson.

It wasn't only the stories, you see, it was the language that was new. My people had come to Australia in 1842 but I may well have been a migrant the way I delighted and tried on my tongue the sounds and fine nuances I'd not heard before. When I found Joseph Conrad twenty years later, I know how he felt with the novelty of a new language. "Read aloud" the preface said and I did. "The cat said, 'you must swear to keep your promise' and the mouse swore to keep the covenant." Every page was so great a thing to me that handling the old worn volume before I sat to write this made me forget my appointments while I read again the things that sent me on journeys and still sends me travelling between covers – some odysseys are physical travel: In 1970 I went 10,000 miles to Ireland, straight to Innisfree. "I will arise and go now, and go to Innisfree, And a small cabin build there, of clay and wattles made . . . I will arise now and go now, for always night and day . . . I hear it in the deep heart's core".

And the first paperbacks I bought myself were in 1946, Homer's *Odyssey* and *Iliad* and then I bought Thucydides, Herodotus and Virgil because THE book had scraped my brain box out and I'd managed to learn Latin, at least to read and write, but nothing I read later impressed me as that first introduction, *The Last Fight in the Coliseum*. Years later when I went to Rome I knew the whole layout of that vast amphitheatre, I'd remembered it.

Almost every one of the scores of poems and stories of that first book I owned affected my future years. Lucian of Samosata's story, inside a whale, written circa 200 AD was so inventive yet almost believable that I later joined the Hakluyt Society to assure myself I'd not miss any great writer of the seas and the men who sail on it.

There was folk lore, faery, rip-snorting adventure such as *Treasure Island;* mystery, William Blake poetry and Francis Thomson, Cervantes and Dean Swift. I met Undine and wept and cried for her – and I haven't told you the half of what was in that goldmine of a book. There was *Pilgrims Progress*, Binyon's For the Fallen, "They went with songs to the battle, they were young . . ."

The preface (which of course I read often as no-one had told me that no-one reads a preface – incidentally I still do) ends: "Goodbye then, dear young reader, I leave you to the treasure. Once you have read . . . no-one can take away from you the joy and the knowledge you will have found" and no-one has.

Claudio Alcorso

1913 – 2000

Claudio Alcorso was an industrialist, winemaker and writer. He was born in Rome in 1938 and emigrated to Sydney and established the firm of Silk and Textile Fabrics. Despite enlisting in the RAAF, he was interned as an 'enemy alien' during the Second World War. He successfully transferred his factory to Derwent Park in Tasmania in 1947. He was a pioneer of the Tasmanian winemaking industry, planting 90 riesling vines at his property Moorilla in the 1950s. He championed the arts through his involvement with the Australian Ballet, Australian Elizabethan Theatre Trust, Tasmanian Arts Advisory Council and as chairman of Opera Australia. He was also a crusader for the environment who took an active stance in 1982 in the Franklin River protest. The Claudio Alcorso Foundation has established an annual Australia–Italy exchange fellowship in his honour. His house in Hobart is now the site of the Museum of Old and New Art.

Please convey to the boys of your Year 11 English class my congratulations for devising a very interesting project.

I was born in Rome and completed my studies through University there. I came to Australia in 1938.

My readings were mostly French authors and Russian. I read the French in the original and the Russian in Italian translation. André Gide, and André Maurois were two of my favourite authors. I remember Dostoievsky as disturbing but not as a profound influence. French writers were investigating "La condition humane", What it means to be human, and when I look back to my young readings this is what comes through. In the same vein Henri Remarque: *A l'Ouest rien de nouveau* created a profound impression. Later, Steinbeck's *Grapes of Wrath.*

I also read in Italian translation Jack London's books of adventure and I loved them.

It seems paradoxical that in writing this letter I cannot mention a book by an Italian author and I am asking myself why is it so. The inescapable answer is that nothing really creative did appear during the fascist period. We read the old authors, but that was part of studying and I do not think they come under your query.

All the above is fairly irrelevant to the question of what books might interest or motivate young Australians today. There is however a great deal of wonderful writing by Anglo-Saxon authors along the same humanistic thinking. I read them later in life.

Charles Anderson, VC

1897 – 1988

Charles Anderson, VC, MC, was born in Cape Town, South Africa, and was educated in Nairobi and at St Brendan's College in Bristol, England, as a boarder. He served as an officer during the East African campaign against the Germans during the First World War, reaching the rank of captain and being awarded the Military Cross. After the war, Anderson settled as a farmer in Kenya. In the early 1930s, he moved to Australia, where he became a grazier. In 1939, he joined the Militia, Australia's part-time military force, before volunteering for overseas service after the outbreak of the Second World War. In early 1941, he was deployed to Malaya as part of the 8th Division, where he rose to command the 2/19th Battalion against the Japanese following their invasion of Malaya in December of that year. For his actions around Muar in January 1942, he was awarded the Victoria Cross before being captured at the end of the fighting on Singapore. He spent over three years in Japanese captivity, before being released at the end of the war. In the post war years, Anderson returned to farming and served as a federal parliamentarian, representing the Division of Hume twice between 1949 and 1961.

The 1914-18 war caught me at a very unfortunate time of life. I was seventeen when the war broke out and I enlisted shortly after the outbreak. Seventeen is an age when one really starts to learn – and to make use of early training "hoe to learn".

I was never lucky enough to have a good English master, other subjects, yes, but not English. I realised later that it was a handicap which had to be overcome.

In the '39-45 war as I became more senior in rank, it was often necessary to write military appreciations and reports in concise unambiguous language – short & clear so that it was easy for tired brains to absorb. I realised then, what a wonderful language English was and sincerely regretted what I missed through lack of early training.

At the ages from 11-13 I read publications like *Chums*, G.A. Hasty's books – stories of adventure, of exploration generally, themes that developed a strong sense of duty, of comradeship and initiative, also an understanding of right & wrong. "The Old School Tie" – never let your friend or your side down.

I progressed to Kipling, I enjoyed his books very much. I understood them very well – from fighting alongside Indian regiments & there was a large Indian settlement in Kenya where I lived from 1900-1935. They taught the importance of national prestige, to the caring of primitive people, responsibility to one's fellow creatures. I had to read Shakespeare for my exams but never appreciated him, just read by rote, it was much later in life, after seeing the play acted I really understood his great worth & why he is to be revered. I had little experience with reading the Classics – a book by Dickens, works of Walter Scott like *Ivanhoe* I liked, Jane Austen – Pride and Prejudice. I developed a lasting preference for romantic novels, the earliest I read was *Under the Red Robe* by Stanley Weyman. I am afraid I neglected my classics and tended to concentrate on authors of romance & chivalry with an occasional biography. Looking back I realised that my reading hampered my development – I do not regret that but I believe I have missed a great deal of enjoyment because my reading was never directed on sounder lines – wider horizons were lost to me.

I hope that what I have written will be of use to you – indeed I rather envy your pupils – you are just 70 years too late for me!

Bob Ansett

Born 1933

Son of Sir Reginald Ansett, Bob Ansett was born in Hamilton, Victoria, and educated at Wesley College and in the United States when his parents divorced and he moved to Alaska with his mother and his brother. In North America he attended the University of Utah with an American Football scholarship. In 1955, he was drafted by the United States Army and served in Japan. By 1965, he was having financial difficulties in the United States and returned to Australia where he established the Budget car rental company. Again, plagued by financial trouble, he was declared bankrupt in 1990. He was chairman of the North Melbourne Football Club from 1978 to 1991.

In response to your letter dated 22 May, I have thought back into my past and recalled the books that perhaps had the greatest impact on me as a youngster, one being Mark Twain's *Huckleberry Finn*.

I suppose the adventure and individual self-reliance had appeal and as time has progressed, I have discovered that I am a very self-reliant individual and this book may have contributed toward it.

There was another series of books written by an American author, whom I have forgotten, but the books were about the *Hardy Boys* and they too were adventurous.*

I also enjoyed any books on aviation and sport but I can't recollect specific books or authors.

*[The *Hardy Boys* books were written by Franklin W. Dixon]

Sir Reginald Ansett

1909 – 1981

Sir Reginald Ansett, KBE, was born in Inglewood, Victoria, and educated at Swinburne Technical College where he trained as a knitting machine technician. He was an enthusiastic private pilot, having obtained his licence in 1926.He ran a road freight business until government regulations prohibited such operations which were in competition with government-owned rail freight services. In 1936 Ansett Airways Pty Ltd inaugurated its first service, from Hamilton to Melbourne using a diminutive six-seater Fokker F.XI Universal. He founded Ansett Transport Industries, which owned one of Australia's two leading domestic. Airlines. He also founded the ATV-0 television station in Melbourne and TVQ-0 in Brisbane which later became part of Network Ten.

From his Public Relations Executive: Sir Reginald Ansett discussed your letter with me and asked me to write to you.

He says the book which gave him the most pleasure and which he has frequently re-read is *The Count of Monte Cristo* by Dumas.

Doug Anthony

1929 – 2020

The Honourable Doug Anthony, AC, CH, was born in Murwillumbah in northern New South Wales and was educated at Murwillumbah Primary School and Murwillumbah High School, before attending The King's School in Sydney and then Gatton College in Queensland. After graduating he took up dairy farming near Murwillumbah. He was elected to the House of Representatives at a 1957 by-election. He was appointed to the ministry in 1964 and in Coalition governments over the following 20 years held a variety of portfolios. He was elected deputy leader of the Country Party in 1964 and succeeded John McEwen as party leader and Deputy Prime Minister in 1971. He retired from politics at the 1984 election.

I have your letter of 22nd May telling me of the project being undertaken by the boys of your Year 11 English class.

I think the books which impressed me most as I was growing up were *Robbery Under Arms* and *Treasure Island*. These are adventurous and exciting stories and I enjoyed the way in which they were written. To this day I enjoy an adventure story and I particularly enjoy a book telling of man's struggle against nature's elements; e.g. *Survive the Savage Antarctic.**

Another book which I enjoyed was the delightfully whimsical *Wind in the Willows*.

*[This could be either *Survive the Savage Sea* by Dougal Robertson or *Endurance: Shackleton's Incredible Voyage* by Alfred Lansing]

Julie Anthony

Born 1949

Julie Anthony AM, OBE, was born in Lamaroo, South Australia. She is a singer and entertainer who is well known for her brief stint as lead singer of the Seekers. A soprano, she has recorded both jazz and pop and is well-known for her live singing performances, variety appearances and roles in cabaret and theatre. She has performed with numerous artists including Simon Gallagher and Anthony Warlow. She recorded an album with jazz performer Don Burrows called "Together at Last". She sang the Australian National Anthem at the Opening Ceremony of the 2000 Sydney Olympics with Human Nature.

Thank you for your letter which caught up with me today in Los Angeles.

Steinbeck's *Grapes of Wrath* stands out for me. As a teenager working on my father's farm in an area not unlike that of the story, & we had great characters as well, fortunately not as tragic as those depicted in the work.

Good luck with your project.

Sir Robert Askin

1907 – 1981

The Honourable Sir Robert Askin, GCMG, was Born in Sydney in 1907. He was educated at Sydney Technical High School. After serving as a bank officer and as a Sergeant in the Second World War, he joined the Liberal Party and was elected to the seat of Collaroy at the 1950 election. He quickly rose through party ranks, eventually becoming Deputy Leader. He remained as Deputy until, after leading the party to a second electoral defeat in 1959, Premier Morton was deposed and Askin was elected to succeed him. At the May 1965 election, he presented the Liberal Party as a viable alternative government. He won a narrow victory, and remained in office for ten years.

I am sorry to be late in replying to your letter of 9th June, but unfortunately, my wife met with a nasty car accident and I have been backwards and forwards to the hospital so much in the last 10 or 12 days that I have not had much time to attend to my correspondence.

However, I can say that I was an avid reader as a youth and can think of quite a few books which influenced me in later years, including of course, the monumental works of William Shakespeare.

If I were called upon to mention just two books, I would say:

> *The Golden Treasury* selected by F.T. Palgrave, which is full of wisdom and enriching thoughts and more especially includes what I, and many other people, believe to be the

most powerful piece in the English language. I refer to Gray's *Elegy* of course – *Written in A Country Churchyard*. It tells the whole story of life and personally I still find it most inspiring. I understand it is the most quoted work of all.

General Woolfe on the heights of Quebec, after defeating the French General, Montcalm, and gaining Canada for Britain when being congratulated, he said he would rather have been the author of Gray's Elegy.

Secondly, and perhaps most importantly from my personal viewpoint, I would nominate *The Story of San Michele*. By Axel Munthe. These memoirs by a practising doctor of medicine, who had fought against plague and disease in many parts of the world, teach one to have compassion for less fortunate people and I am glad to say it certainly influenced me in various items of Social Legislation put on the Statute Book in this State during my 10 years as Premier.

I hope these comments may be of some use to you and congratulate the boys in your Year on having devised such a thoughtful and what should be rewarding project.

Sir Garfield Barwick

1903 - 1997

The Right Honourable Sir Garfield Barwick, AK, KCMG, was Australia's longest serving Chief Justice of the High Court from 1964 to 1981. He was educated at Fort Street High School and the University of Sydney where he graduated with a Bachelor of Laws degree and the University Medal in Law. He was called to the Bar in 1927 and had a highly successful career as a barrister prior to entering the House of Representatives as Member for Parramatta in 1958. He was initially appointed Attorney-General and later added Minister for External Affairs to his responsibilities. He also served as President of the Australian Conservation Foundation.

You certainly tax my recollection when you ask me to nominate a book favoured by me as a teenager. You realise that that is more than sixty years ago.

I was interested in adventure stories, particularly if they had any historical content. A book, still on my shelves, which comes to mind is *Wulf the Saxon*. This book had historical interest because it concerned an important stage in early English history. It had its moments of excitement. The courage of its hero pleased me. Also, the story brought home to me, on the one hand, the near primitive conditions of the time and, on the other hand, the continuing similarity of human motives and emotions notwithstanding the changing environments to be found in the development of human society.

Marjorie Barnard

1897 – 1987

Marjorie Barnard, OAM, was born in Sydney and educated at the Cambridge School, Sydney Girls High School and the University of Sydney where she graduated with first class honours and the University Medal in History. She was offered a scholarship to Oxford but her father refused her permission to go so she trained as a librarian at Sydney Teachers' College. She worked as a librarian until 1935 when she gave it away go concentrate on writing.

She met her collaborator, Flora Eldershaw, at the University of Sydney, and they published their first novel, "A House is Built" in 1929. Their collaboration spanned the next two decades, and covered the full range of their writing: fiction, history and literary criticism. They published under the pseudonym M. Barnard Eldershaw. Marjorie Barnard was a significant part of the literary scene in Australia between the wars and, for both her work as M. Barnard Eldershaw and in her own right, is recognised as a major figure in Australian letters.

Her most successful fictional work written in her own right is "The Persimmon Tree and Other Stories" published in 1943. It was reissued in 1985, with the inclusion of three additional stories not previously published in book form. The title story, "The Persimmon Tree", is one of Australia's most anthologised stories. After Eldershaw's death, Barnard continued to write, mostly histories and literary criticism, including, in 1967, the first biography of Miles Franklin. Her "History of Australia", was published in 1963.

Your letter of 6th June reached me to-day. A letter from Melbourne to Point Clare usually takes eight days, seventeen days, even if re-routed from Longueville, is abnormal. The postal service in rural suburbia cannot be described as dedicated. This explains my delay in answering. Your class project is interesting and I am happy to co-operate.

Two books made a deep and lasting impression on me long ago when I was about fourteen.

1. Merezhkovsky's *The Forerunner*. In it I saw the full blaze of the Renaissance and it had the force of a personal experience. It was more than the story of Leonardo, it was a mass miracle. Humanity had a growing point.

2. Voltaire's *Philosophic Dictionary*. After school I had half an hour or so to spare before I caught my ferry home. I spent it in Angus & Robertson's book shop in Castlereagh St. opposite the school. I had heard of Voltaire. I began to read & was fascinated. Religion was a troubled subject in my home. I was confused. In the *Dictionary* I found a lucid and compelling philosophy. I became a rationalist on the spot. I had nearly finished reading it when the copy was sold. My feet were, for a time anyway, on firm ground.

Best wishes & I hope you have a good catch.

John Béchervaise

1910 – 1998

John Béchervaise, MBE, OAM, was born in Melbourne and educated at Melbourne Teachers' College and later at the Courtauld Institute of Art in London. He joined The Geelong College in 1935 in order to establish a program of outdoor activities for the boys. In the 1950s he joined the Australian National Antarctic Research Expeditions. He served as field leader on Heard Island in 1953, leading an unsuccessful expedition to climb the 2745 m Mawson Peak of the Big Ben massif, the highest peak on Australian territory. He also served as station leader at Mawson Station, Antarctica in 1955 and 1959. He returned to the Antarctic on MV Nanok S on her first trip south with ANARE in the summer of 1979–80. He was a highly respected teacher at Geelong Grammar School during the 1960s and early 1970s. As well as contributing to the development of outdoor education in Victoria, he was for many years the assistant editor of the Australian magazine "Walkabout".

Your note has arrived at almost the moment of my departure for America, and I must, perhaps, answer very much 'off the cuff' . . .

In my youth I was fortunate in being able to browse through two very considerable private libraries – that of my father – which contained numerous volumes on the explorers – including, inevitably the lives and expeditions of men like Robert Falcon Scott. His library also included a number of old anthologies and 'readers' – such as the old 'Royal Readers' and in these I buried myself very often. I even enjoyed much of his taste in verse – the Australians . . . and Rudyard Kipling. But, even when I went walking in the bush, I often took Kipling's *Rewards and Fairies* and *Puck of Pooks Hill*, to say nothing of the Jungle Books. Rider Haggard became a great favourite – all his African books. And I pored over the Brigadier Gerrard series . . . Lastly, my faulty memory, reaches back to two volumes which my own great-great-grandfather wrote, of his experiences on Jersey, in the fur-trading outposts of Canada, and, later, in the Royal Navy, as Master of a privateer, and later on men-of-war.

My grandfather's library was of an historian and, in addition to what I suppose were the usual standard works, he had a wonderful library of art – painting, architecture, sculpture. In his library I spent much time, and became very familiar with most of the 'old masters' and with the painting of the nineteenth century. I must have been a prig, and highly prejudiced. My grandfather, Robert Mayston, was a considerable Shakespeare scholar and, certainly in my later 'teens, I enjoyed his quotations, and eventually found them for myself.

In the final analysis I believe that I got more from the libraries of my youth than I got from school – though I was quite fond of the schools and teachers of my youth. My subsequent career, first in teaching and art history, and later in exploration and writing, was certainly pre-set by my early reading. Good luck with your project.

Sir Joh Bjelke-Petersen

1911 - 2005

The Hon. Sir Johannes Bjelke-Petersen, KCMG, was born in Dannevirke, New Zealnd, and came to Australia with his family in 1913. He was a farmer and a conservative politician and was the longest-serving premier of Queensland, holding office from 1968 to 1987, during which time the state underwent considerable economic development. He was one of the most well-known and controversial figures of 20th-century Australian politics because of his uncompromising conservatism (including his role in the downfall of the Whitlam federal government), political longevity, and the institutional corruption of his government.

I have your letter of 22nd May, 1980, wherein you ask "which book or books were your favourites or influenced you most as a teenager and why?"

In response, might I say that the Bible and books of famous people in all walks of life were read by me with a great deal of interest. I had a particular interest in books about men who had achieved much such as Edison and Ford.

I trust that the foregoing is what you require.

Geoffrey Blainey

Born 1930

Professor Geoffrey Blainey, AC, was born in Melbourne and educated at Wesley College. In 1961, he began teaching economic history at the University of Melbourne, was made a professor in 1968, and was given the Ernest Scott chair in history in 1977. In 1982, he was appointed dean of Melbourne's Faculty of Arts. From 1994 to 1998, Blainey was foundation Chancellor of the University of Ballarat. He was visiting professor of Australian Studies at Harvard University. He is noted for having written authoritative texts on the economic and social history of Australia, including "The Tyranny of Distance", "Captain Cook's Epic Voyages", "Wesley College: The First Hundred Years" and "A Land Half Won". He has published over 40 books, including wide-ranging histories of the world and of Christianity.

Thanks for your letter about the 11th year English class. I'm not sure if I can give a sensible answer. Between the ages of say 13and 16 I read a few hundred books, I imagine. I got enormous pleasure and stimulus out of them – travel books, novels, histories. I'm not sure that I know which were my favourites, because I did not read any book more than once. I suspect too that the books which gave me the most pleasure were not classics but well-told contemporary stories.

When I was about fourteen I read some exciting personal books about the Boer War but I can't remember their names. I think one was called *Commando,* by Deneys Reitz. I got great pleasure out of some of Bernard Shaw's political writings when I was about fifteen – *Everybody's Political What's What* must have been one such book. I was excited too by his preface to *Back to Methuselah* – not that I properly understood it. One of the classic novels Thomas Hardy's *The Mayor of Casterbridge* pleased me. Not many Australian books seemed to be around then. Walter Murdoch's life of Alfred Deakin stimulated me. Some books I liked for the sound of their prose as much as their meaning. Sorry I can't be more helpful.

There was a great vogue for humorous books called *William* books written by Richmal Crompton. We devoured them but that was possibly between the ages of 9 and 12 – I forget which.

I have been in China, so the reply is late. Best wishes.

John Blight

1913 – 1995

Born in Unley, South Australia, John Blight, AM, was educated at Brisbane State High School. During the Great Depression in Australia he tramped the Queensland outback looking for work. In the 1930s he undertook correspondence studies and attained his Chartered Accountancy Diploma, and in 1939 he began work in Bundaberg, Queensland.

Following his wartime years spent in Canberra as an Inspector with the Government's Prices Regulatory Department, he became a part-owner of timber mills in the Gympie region. He took up full-time writing in 1973.

He received numerous awards, including the Dame Mary Gilmore Medal, Grace Leven Prize for Poetry, The Patrick White Literary Award and the Christopher Brennan Award.

Endeavouring go remember over fifty years ago, I believe that in my very early 'teens, the book which I first held in memory was Rudyard Kipling's *Stalky & Co.*

Reaching my mid-'teens I read Fennimore Cooper's novels with avidity after which I seemed to wish for some reading a little heavier and read Lord Bulwer-Lytton's novels, with a special interest in his *The Last Days of Pompeii.*

About the age of 16 years I began to include much poetry in my reading and was particularly attracted to the Lake Poets. Wordsworth was my first fancy and I immediately took to

Coleridge's *The Rime of the Ancient Mariner* as it appeared in a volume of his Poetical Works which I still possess.

However my reading quickly spread over a much wider field in my late 'teens and there were so many good books that they fused into a general liking to read philosophical, historical and scientific works besides ancient mythologies and translations of Eastern religious tracts including *The Koran*.

Sir Henry Bolte

1908 – 1990

The Honourable Sir Henry Bolte, GCMG, was Premier of Victoria from 1955 to 1972. He was born in Ballarat and attended Skipton State School and Ballarat Grammar School and was a farmer before being elected to the Victorian Parliament as the Member for Hampden in 1947, becoming leader of the Liberal Party in 1953. His term as Premier was a record 17 years.

When at school in my early teens I read everything that had a relationship to British history, much of course part fact & part fiction. This habit or fancy has stayed with me. I have always enjoyed this type of book & believe that I have received a great benefit from them. A desire to serve one's Crown & Country being a byproduct.

Sir Jack Brabham

1926 – 2014

Sir Jack Brabham AO, OBE, was born in Hurstville, New South Wales, and educated at Hurstville Public School and Kogarah Technical School. He was an RAAF flight mechanic and ran a small engineering workshop before he started racing midget cars in 1948. His successes with midgets in Australian and New Zealand road-racing events led to his going to Britain to further his racing career. There he became part of the Cooper Car Company's racing team, building as well as racing cars. He contributed to the design of the mid-engined cars that Cooper introduced to Formula One and the Indianapolis 500, and won the Formula One world championship in 1959 and 1960. In 1962 he established his own Brabham marque which in the 1960s became the largest manufacturer of custom racing cars in the world. In the 1966 Formula One season Brabham became the first – and still, the only – man to win the Formula One world championship driving one of his own cars.

Thank you for your letter of May 22nd which unfortunately arrived whilst I was in England, hence the delay in reply.

On reflection, as a boy my favourite books were *Treasure Island* and *Robinson Crusoe*. While I couldn't say if either influenced my life in any way, I do like to do things in my own way and to be independent whenever possible, so perhaps *Robinson Crusoe* did have some effect.

Good luck with your project and best wishes to yourself and the boys.

John Brack

1900 - 1999

John Brack was an Australian painter, and a member of the Antipodeans group. According to one critic, Brack's early works captured the idiosyncrasies of their time "more powerfully and succinctly than any Australian artist before or since. Brack forged the iconography of a decade on canvas as sharply as Barry Humphries did on stage." During World War 2 he served with the Field Artillery. He was Art Master at Melbourne Grammar School from 1952 to 1962 when he was appointed Head of National Gallery of Victoria Art School from 1962 to 1968, where he was an influence on many artists and the creation of the expanded school attached to the new gallery building. His early conventional style evolved into one of simplified, almost stark, shapes and areas of deliberately drab colour, often featuring large areas of brown. He made an initial mark in the 1950s with works on the contemporary Australian culture, such as the iconic Collins St., 5 pm, a view of rush hour in post-war Melbourne.

As a teenager I read a good deal, and I believe I was as much overwhelmed by *War and Peace, The Brothers Karamazov*, and *The Wasteland* as anyone else of my generation. But if I had to select one book which influenced me more than any others, it would be a quite minor work, Auden and MacNeice's *Letters from Iceland* which I came upon in 1937 at the age of 17. It was the first book which gave me the sensation that it was directed at me personally. The names were unknown to me then, but the tone, in particular that of Auden's verses was just what I'd instinctively been looking for: cerebral, elegant, cool without solemnity, free from rhetorical flourishes (which I felt appeared even in T.S. Eliot), seeking for truth, but above all showing an attitude of scepticism towards Romanticisms which came as a revelation to me.

Indeed the subsequent poems and essays of Auden may have been the strongest of all intellectual influences upon my formative years.

Russell Braddon

1921 – 1995

Russell Braddon was born in North Sydney and educated at Sydney Grammar School and the University of Sydney. Shortly after graduating, he joined the army and served in the Malayan campaign during World War II. He was held as a prisoner of war by the Japanese in Pudu and Changi prisons and on the Thailand-Burma Railway between 1942 and 1945. His chronicle of his four years as a prisoner of war, "The Naked Island", sold more than a million copies and was one of the first accounts of a Japanese prisoner of war's experience.

He went on to produce a wide range of works, including novels, biographies, histories, TV scripts and newspaper articles. In addition, he was a frequent broadcaster on British radio and television.

Herewith my doubtless unsatisfactory answer to your question.

I didn't have a favourite author as a teenager. I read everything available – from Dornford Yates to Sapper, Agatha Christie to P.G. Wodehouse to Sir Philip Gibbs. But I didn't like the classics. Most teenagers, I believe, don't. I liked books that spoke to my eye in my own idiom about my own times. I liked the private pleasure & the solitary adventure simply of "reading". I hope it's a pleasure & adventure not being denied to today's teenagers – either by themselves or by anyone else – from their teachers to their contemporaries – because it's just about the only one that lasts an entire life-time.

Sir Donald Bradman

1908 – 2001

Sir Donald Bradman, AC, was born in Cootamundra and grew up in Bowral where he attended Bowral Intermediate High School. He developed his hand-eye coordination by spending hours hitting a golf ball against a water tank with a cricket stump. He played cricket for New South Wales from 1927 to 1934, for South Australia from 1935 to 1949 and for Australia from 1928 to 1948, finishing his Test career with an average of 99.94 runs. He was Chairman of the Australian Board of Control for International Cricket from 1960 to 1963 and served on the boards of a number of companies. Considered the best batsman in the history of the game, he was also an excellent golfer.

As a teenager I cannot remember reading books of any consequence. This is contrary to what has been written about me but I am not responsible for the inaccuracies of authors.

Partly because of my experience I am a great advocate of youngsters reading as much as they can. I realise how much I would have helped in this way.

John Bray

1912– 1995

Despite describing himself as a Bohemian with an unconventional temperament, John Bray, AC, QC, was considered to be one of the country's most capable judges. He was born in Wayville, South Australia, and educated at Mrs Hill's School in Glenelg, as a border at St Peter's College and the University of Adelaide where he graduated with a Bachelor of Laws degree with Honours and later as a Doctor of Laws. Following practice as a solicitor, he was called to the Bar in 1933 and became a Queen's Counsel in 1957. He was a member of the Libraries Board of South Australia from 1944 to 1989. Appointed Chief Justice of the Supreme Court of South Australia in 1967, he remained in that post until 1978. He was Chancellor of the University of Adelaide from 1968 to 1983. A writer all his life, he published six books of poetry, two plays and two works of non-fiction.

My response may be disconcerting. I had an old-fashioned education. The books I encountered at school and at the University were textbooks and the classics. Twentieth century literature when I was at school meant Kipling and Masefield. I don't remember any Australian books at all apart from Australian history. It was not until I left school for some time that I heard of James Joyce, D.H. Lawrence or T.S. Eliot.

I do not regret this. I hold strongly the view that contemporary literature should form no part of the school curriculum. It should be encountered naturally outside the school like other contemporary phenomena, not converted into a school text. It should not need the teacher to mediate between it and the reader. On the other hand if the pupil is not introduced to the great works of the past at school he or she may never encounter them at all.

I was very fond of Scott. My favourite novel of his was, I think, and still is *Redgauntlet*. I was of course, greatly impressed and moved by Shakespeare. I liked and still like many of the poems in such anthologies as Palgrave's *Golden Treasury*. At school, I was introduced to Virgil (the *Anaeid*) and the Odes of Horace. They impressed me then and much more in later life. After I left school I encountered other Latin authors, notably Catullus, and taught myself Greek. I read Gibbon's *Decline and Fall of the Roman Empire* when I was about seventeen and that imbued me with a lasting interest in Roman history.

Of course I read much ephemeral stuff for entertainment but I cannot say that it left any enduring impression on my mind.

Hence my tastes were clearly set in classic moulds. They have so remained. I am not sorry about any of this. Re-reading this I think I have used the word encounter too many times and given an unintended impression of pedantry and pride. I apologize for this. But let it stand.

Niall Brennan

1918 – 2005

Born in Melbourne and educated at St Kevin's College and the University of Melbourne, Niall Brennan was a prolific writer. He worked in the Ministry of Information and Radio during the Second World War and with the War Organisation of Industry. In 1943, he published "The Ballad of a Government Man", "The Making of a Moron" in 1954, "A Hoax Called Jones" in 1963. Two biographies followed, one in 1964 of Dr Mannix, who was the Catholic Archbishop, of Melbourne and the second in 1971 of John Wren. "Men and War" appeared in 1972 and a history of Nunawading in 1972. "Tales from the Australian Mountains" was published in 1980 and a biography of wartime cameraman Damien Parer in 1994.

It is not easy to recall with accuracy the books that moved me in my teens; but I will have a stab at it.

My father was devoted to French authors and I read much of Victor Hugo and Anatole France; numerous stories by the latter, some of them novelettes, but specifically *The Laughing Man* and *Les Miserables* by Hugo. I enjoyed them so much that I have never wanted to re-read in case the magic of them was dissipated by cynical old age.

Graham Greene was just emerging. I enjoyed Evelyn Waugh's satires. As a young Catholic "intellectual" I read a great deal of G.K. Chesterton and Hilaire Belloc, but not unfortunately their opposite numbers, Wells and Shaw. I enjoyed Shaw's plays, read nothing of Wells.

I read all of John Galsworthy's plays and loved them. Not his books, just his plays. They made *Loyalties* into a film and I was so entranced by it that I dragged my father to see it. He enjoyed the film too, being a Galsworthy fan.

My grandfather and my father both had big libraries. I have inherited them both, plus libraries from uncles and aunts, friends and acquaintances and I now have what must be one of the biggest private libraries I have ever seen. So my children are carrying on.

I think in adolescence you are becoming aware of social problems and issues, and that might be a thread common to all of those books mentioned.

Sir Macfarlane Burnet

1899 - 1985

Sir Macfarlane Burnet, OM, AK, KBE, FRS, was born in Traralgon, Victoria, and educated at The Geelong College. He graduated in medicine at the University of Melbourne and completed his PhD at the University of London. He went on to conduct pioneering research in microbiology and immunology at the Walter and Eliza Hall Institute of Medical Research, Melbourne, and served as director of the Institute from 1944 to 1965. From 1965 until his retirement in 1978, Burnet worked at the University of Melbourne. Throughout his career he played an active role in the development of public policy for the medical sciences in Australia and was a founding member of the Australian Academy of Science and served as its president from 1965 to 1969. He won a Nobel Prize in 1960 for predicting acquired immune tolerance and he developed the theory of clonal selection.

A brief answer to your question on teenage reading.

In my case the preferred and most influential author was H.G. Wells. I started the same fiction stories very early and continued reading almost every book of his until the time of his death. He had an enormous influence on my thinking.

G.K. Chesterton was also a favourite – The other area of interest was natural history – I read whatever came my way - J.H. Fabres insect books, Frogatt's *Australian Insects*, the *Harmsworth Natural History* in weekly parts – and David McDonald's column in *The Argus*.

I hope this is helpful.

Jim Cairns

1914 - 2003

Jim Cairns was born in Carlton and attended Northcote High School where he was a good student and athlete. He joined the Victoria Police and studied at night, graduating with a Bachelor of Economics degree from the University of Melbourne. He left the police force and lectured in economic history at the university. Elected to Federal Parliament in 1955, he completed a doctorate in economic history and became Minister for Secondary Industry in the Whitlam Labor government. He was appointed Deputy Prime Minister and Treasurer in 1974. A writer throughout his life, he was author of more than 20 books.

When I was a teenager, I read virtually nothing at all in the way of memorable or influential books. It was not until I was in my twenties that I began reading seriously. It was then that I read Henry George's *Progress and Poverty* which is still a socially and historically significant book. The author was something of a 'character' and he once ran for the post of Mayor of New York. His ideas enjoyed a considerable following in the latter part of the 19ᵗʰ century and the early part of the 20ᵗʰ. Some of George's more doctrinaire or dogmatic followers see in *Progress and Poverty* the answers to the world's problems.

Clive Caldwell

1911 - 1994

Clive Caldwell, DSO, DFC & Bar, was born in the Sydney suburb of Lewisham and educated at Albion Park School, Sydney Grammar School and Trinity Grammar School. He learned to fly in 1938 with the Royal Aero Club of New South Wales. He was employed as a commission agent when World War II broke out, and he joined the Citizen Air Force of the RAAF in 1940, with the intention of becoming a fighter pilot and joined the Empire Air Training Scheme. He is officially credited with shooting down 28.5 enemy aircraft in over 300 operational sorties. In addition to his official score, he has been ascribed six probables and 15 damaged. He flew Curtiss P-40 Tomahawks and Kittyhawks in the North African Campaign and Supermarine Spitfires in the South West Pacific Theatre. He was the highest-scoring P-40 pilot from any air force and the highest-scoring Allied pilot in North Africa.

Having been away I've not until now had the opportunity to reply to your letter.

In the period under review, I was enthralled by accounts of the aerial operational engagements of such greats as Mannock, Bishop, Fonck, Udet, McCudden, Collishaw, Richthofen, Guynemer and others in the then recent war in the air.

It seemed to me that there could be nothing to be more desired than to be as they, the single seater day fighter pilots – the true elite.

When opportunity offered in the later greater war this thought so strongly persisted that I was at pains to qualify for the chance to practice the art myself and experience all that went with it.

It is also proper to mention here what a deep impression was made on me by the clearly stated quality of content of the funeral oration of Pericles which I specially commend to the attention of your class.

Dame Carmen Callil

Born 1938

Publisher, writer, critic and broadcaster, Dame Carmen Callil, DBE, was born in Melbourne and educated at Star of the Sea, Loreto Mandeville Hall and the University of Melbourne where she graduated with a Bachelor of Arts degree. After working for a number of publishers in the UK, she founded Virago Press in 1972. She was Managing Director of Chatto & Windus and Hogarth Press from 1982 to 1993 and Editor at Large at Alfred Knopf, Pantheon and Vintage in the USA from 1993 to 1994. She published "Bad Faith: A Forgotten History of Family and Fatherland" in 2006.

Off the top of my head these favourites come to mind:

Persuasion by Jane Austen. I always identify with losers and Anne almost does, until the end. Also, I love the way Jane Austen writes and the England she described seemed a far away and magic land to me when I was young.

Kidnapped by Robert Louis Stevenson. I used to read this book over and over again. Difficult to know why – perhaps because once again it was set far away and because the hero escaped to greater things. I also very much like the prose of Robert Louis Stevenson.

All Richmal Crompton's *William* books. These possibly because my brother used to make me pay a shilling to read them if I wanted to. Also they made me laugh.

Finally, Simone de Beauvoir's *Memoirs of a Dutiful Daughter* which someone gave me for my 18th birthday (is that still adolescence?) and which changed my life.

My favourite Australian book was and still is Joseph Furphy's *Such is Life* although I wish someone had given me *My Brilliant Career* by Miles Franklin, which I would have loved differently, but just as much.

Sir Roderick Carnegie

Born 1932

Sir Roderick Carnegie, AC, was born in Melbourne and was educated at Geelong Grammar School, the University of Melbourne, Oxford University and Harvard University. In 1958 he became a consultant with McKinsey & Company in the United States, in 1963 he founded the Australian practice of McKinsey in Melbourne, and in 1967 he returned to New York to become a Director of the Company. He subsequently joined CRA Limited (now Rio Tinto) as Finance Director in 1972, served as Managing Director from 1974 to 1986, and as Chairman. Since 1986, he has served as a director of several companies, including the Australian Advisory Board of General Motors, CSIRO, Business Council of Australia, Group of Thirty and was Chairman of the Advisory Committee on Relations with Japan.

Thank you for your letter. I strongly believe that an addiction to far-ranging reading habits should be acquired if possible from early childhood.

As a young teenager in Melbourne, I grew up in a community that knew itself in peril, was at war, and achieved a common consensus. I read avidly, as did everyone, the skimpy newspapers of the day. There are few new books in wartime. There was no television, and radio was very different from what it is today. So we read widely, and willingly, whatever we could. For me, the first long delight of reading came from the novels of Walter Scott. Historical novels stimulated the imagination and gave me a sense of history. I also learnt to read fast because they were long books.

Thirty years on, Winston Churchill's *History of the English Speaking Peoples* still remains on my re-reading list. That book, written by a politician who had apparently failed but finally emerged as a world leader, impressed on me that history and biography can teach lessons of real present and future relevance.

In teenage, I had no thought of business or of mining. I had vague ambitions of a career on the family property, or as a scientist; and it was in science that I first graduated from Melbourne. But I have always tried to read widely, if possible every night, about the world we live in and our fellow human beings.

TV has its occasional triumphs, but so much of every evening is manufactured make-believe, or superficial and trivial. For each hour in front of "the box", why not give a matching hour with a book? One good book, let alone your school or local library, contains enjoyment, excitement, or food for maturing thought. If it is from your own shelf, with other books to which you can return again and again, that is even better. It is by reflection that we learn.

Matt Carroll

Born 1944

Matt Carroll was born in Sydney and educated at the University of New South Wales where he graduated with the degree of Bachelor of Architecture. He joined the South Australian Film Corporation in 1973 where he produced feature films, television programs and documentaries. His best-known films include "Storm Boy", "Sunday Too Far Away" and "Breaker Morant". In 1982, he joined Network Ten, taking responsibility for the network's drama productions. In 1985, he and Greg Coote formed Roadshow which produced "Brides of Christ". Ten years later, he formed his own production company.

As I started reading at a very early age and have continued to read a wide range of books ever since, your question is a bit of a curly one.

There was certainly not one individual book which influenced me. However, the following I do remember more vividly than others: *The Foundation and Empire* – trilogy by Isaac Asimov; *Fountainhead* by Ayn Rand; the complete short stories of Somerset Maugham; and *David Copperfield* by Charles Dickens.

Maie Casey

1891 – 1983

Lady Casey, AC, was born in Brunswick, Melbourne, where she was educated privately before being sent as a boarder to St George's Shool in the UK and then finishing school in Paris. Following the outbreak of the Great War, she worked in a hospital for wounded officers. She married Richard Casey (later Lord Casey) in 1926. She and her husband both learnt to fly and later constructed an airstrip on their property at Berwick. She accompanied her husband to the USA in 1940 and Cairo in 1942 then to Canberra when her husband was elected to parliament and later appointed Governor-General. She published "An Australian Story 1837-1907" in 1965 and "Tides and Eddies" in 1966.

As all my forebears came to Australia in the 1830s I was primarily interested in history – bits and pieces, family letters.

My brother who was much older than I left behind in our library such desirable books as *Chums* and volumes of *The Boys Own Annual* illustrated by the wonderful artist Hardy.

As I was French speaking from the age of five, much of my reading was in French and I became interested in the works of Balzac and later of Marcel Proust, and any available books on Napoleon 1.

Illustrated notebooks of my great-grandfather John Cotton (1802-49) some of which were recently published by William Collins as *Birds of the Port Phillip District of New South Wales 1843–1849.*

Nancy Cato

1917 – 2000

Nancy Cato, AM, was born in Glen Osmond in South Australia. She studied English literature and Italian at the University of Adelaide, graduating in 1939, then completed a two-year course at the South Australian School of Arts. She was a cadet journalist on "The News" from 1935 to 1941, and an art critic from 1957 to 1958.

She edited the 1950 "Jindyworobak Anthology", one of a series of anthologies produced to promote indigenous Australian ideas and customs, particularly in poetry. Her most famous work is her trilogy, known as "All the Rivers Run". It was originally published as three separate volumes: "All the Rivers Run" in 1958, "Time, Flow Softly" in1959 and "But Still the Stream" in 1962. They were published in one volume in 1971 and made into a TV mini-series "All the Rivers Run", which was broadcast in 1983. She is also known for her work campaigning on environmental and conservation issues.

"Teenager" covers a good many years, from thirteen to nineteen, and my tastes obviously changed in this time; I graduated from *The Schoolgirls' Own* to Tolstoy. *War and Peace* remains one of my favourite books, because of its sweep of characters in space and time: a vast canvas, yet full of intimate human detail.

At sixteen, when I was doing Leaving English (in which I got top credit for the State of S.A.) our set novel was Thomas Hardy's *The Return of the Native*. It is still one of my favourite books and I have read it several times. It sent me to other Hardy novels, *Jude*

the Obscure, Tess of the d'Urbervilles, The Mayor of Casterbridge.
In that year I also read his long historical-philosophical poem,
The Dynasts, dealing with the Napoleonic Wars. The first and last
of these titles influenced my whole philosophy of life, or perhaps
confirmed what I was already beginning to feel: a pessimistic
view of the human condition.

As a younger teenager my favourite book was *Lorna Doone* which
my father had won as a school prize years before. To me it was
exciting, romantic, exotic in a way no Australian novel could be.
It was many years before I discovered William Gosse Hay's novel
Escape of the Notorious Sir William Means set in Tasmania.

Donald Charlwood

1915 - 2012

Donald Charlwood, AM, was born in Melbourne and grew up in Frankston where he attended Frankston High School. In 1933, he took a job on a family friend's farm at Nareen in south-west Victoria. While working there, he completed a short-story course by correspondence with the London School of Journalism and had a number of stories published. When World War 2 broke out, he joined the RAAF and, after training in Australia and Canada, he was posted to Bomber Command as a navigator. Following his return to Australia he was invalided out of the RAAF in July 1945 with back trouble. He commenced work with the Department of Civil Aviation, initially as an Air Traffic Controller, and later in training and recruitment. It was while working at the DCA that he wrote "No Moon Tonight", published in 1956, relying heavily on diaries he kept during training and operational flying. "No Moon Tonight" and "Journeys into Night" published in 1991 have been described as among the finest autobiographical works on Bomber Command in World War 2. "All the Green Year", published in 1965, has been described as a perceptive observation of Australian childhood. The book sold more than 100,000 copies and there were 21 editions between 1965 and 1983. It was made into a television series in 1980 and features in the anthology, "The Australian Collection: Australia's Greatest Books".

My apologies for the delay in answering your query of June 9 concerning my favourite books as a 'teenager'. (No doubt I was once a 'teenager' but it was then an unrecognized category of human being!)

Although light fiction – Sabatini, Farnol, D.K. Broster – and boys' periodicals now long dead, did absorb me in my 'teens, I don't think I was really influenced by a book until we studied *Kidnapped* in Form 2. I had earlier read *Treasure Island* and had enjoyed it immensely, but now a good English teacher opened my eyes to Stevenson's technique – his spare prose; his preference for strong verbs and nouns over adjectives; his telling similes. Analysing his technique did not at all spoil the book for me – I already wanted to write and was soon trying to imitate Stevenson. Of course, I was led to read others of his books.

Our set novel in the next year appealed to me even more – but not as something to attempt to imitate. It was *David Copperfield* and we rollicked through it with an even better teacher. (That was in 1930 and, happily, I am still able to visit the teacher.) I have used this reading of *David Copperfield* in a fictitious way in *All the Green Year*. The crowded life of the book and the extraordinary assortment of characters absorbed me. Even more, I was very much carried into David's troubled life. Recently I re-read the storm scene – when Steerforth is drowned – and was as impressed by it as ever.

I recognize now an influence I was unaware of as a boy: the King James version of the *Book of Common Prayer*. Its cadences and imagery and arrangement of words appealed to me even when I was scarcely aware of meanings! I hope these few remarks will fill your need.

Manning Clark

1915 – 1991

Professor Manning Clark, AC, was born in Sydney and educated at State Schools at Cowes and Belgrave, Melbourne Grammar School, the University of Melbourne and Oxford University. He was at Oxford when war broke out in 1939 but he was unfit for military service. He began teaching and coaching cricket at Blundell's School. In June 1940 he returned to Australia, abandoning his unfinished thesis, but was unable to get a teaching position at an Australian university due to the wartime decline in enrolments. Instead, he taught history at Geelong Grammar School until 1944, and also coached the school's First XI. He lectured in political science at the University of Melbourne from 1944 to 1946 and history from 1946 to 1948. Between 1962 and 1987 he published his six-volume "A History of Australia". In 1980, he was named Australian of the Year. His last works were two volumes of autobiography, "The Puzzles of Childhood" published in 1989 and "The Quest for Grace" published in 1990. A third, unfinished volume, "A Historian's Apprenticeship" was published after his death.

Thank you for your letter of 11 June.

At the risk of appearing to be QUAINT I am going to say that the book which influenced me most in all my childhood was HYMNS ANCIENT AND MODERN. That probably transpired because I was a clergyman's son. I was over exposed to it. I found some of the words very PUZZLING, some unintentionally very funny, but some DEEPLY moving – indeed so moving that it would be difficult to refer in public to such hymns as ABIDE WITH ME, of SUN OF MY SOUL, or NOW THE DAY IS OVER without a CATCH in the voice. I was also influenced by the PSALMS. Thinking back over the years I like to think they INTIMATED the reasons for not being carried away by the FACILE surmises in some hymns, or the narrow British view of the world which was DRILLED into us at school. But, then, who can tell what turns the mind in a child to think about the things that matter in life?

Sir Rupert Clarke

1919 – 2005

Sir Rupert Clarke, 3rd Baronet, AM, MBE was born in Sydney. His father purchased a villa in Monte Carlo and Rupert attended a French-speaking primary school. His father died when Rupert was seven. His mother re-married and moved to England where Rupert was educated at Eton College and Oxford University. By 1941 he had enlisted in the British Army and was commissioned in the Irish Guards, as aide-de-camp to Lieutenant-General Sir Harold Alexander. He was present at various major turning points in the war, including the withdrawal from Burma, the North African Campaign against the German Afrika Korps and the Invasion of Sicily. He imported King Ranch cattle to Australia and he established his own stud herd. He became involved in horse racing, and was on the Victoria Amateur Turf Club (now the Melbourne Racing Club) for 40 years, nearly half that time as chairman. He was also chairman of Cadbury Schweppes Australia, and P&O Australia, deputy chairman of the Distillers Group and the third generation of Clarke baronets to sit on the board of the National Australia Bank. He was also the Honorary Consul of Monaco.

Thank you for your letter of July 4 and I was encouraged by your intention to assist and improve the reading habits of boys at your school.

For what it is worth, the book which probably had the most influence on me at that age was *The Poems of Adam Lindsay Gordon* which I was given when I was about 14/15. This book continuously reminded me of the real Australia and the attributes of an Australian.

I hope that this book will be read and known to the boys in your class as I think it is just as important today as it was many years ago.

Jon Cleary

1917 – 2010

Prolific thriller writer Jon Cleary had no less than nine of his novels made into films. He was born in Sydney and educated at Marist College, Ashgrove, and Marcellin College, Randwick. He left school at 14 and worked in a range of jobs before joining the AIF early in World War II, serving in the Middle East and in New Guinea. He published 53 books, notably "The Sundowners", "You Can't See 'Round Corners" and 20 in the series about fictional Sydney detective Scobie Malone.

Which books influenced me most as a teenager? To a man of 63, that is like asking him which tunes he whistled in those days – I remember now; it was

St Louis Blues, very appropriate for the Depression – or which girl he fell in love with every Saturday night – sorry, I can't remember those.

I left school just before my 15th birthday and was in and out of work for the rest of my teens – so I had plenty of time for reading at the local library. I remember in my late teens I was very taken with Joseph Conrad, though to be truthful it was many years later before I appreciated the depth of what he was trying to say. I also discovered Graham Greene long before he became the cult figure he is now. At that time I had no idea of being a writer – I just wanted to read, to escape from Coogee, the suburb where I lived. I had no money to travel – if it had cost two shillings to go round the world, I couldn't have got out of sight (an old gag) – and so I took the library road.

I've always liked to laugh and I read P.G. Wodehouse – and can't read him now; has my sense of humour changed? – and Stephen Leacock and Mark Twain – and I still read him and still laugh as much as I used to. It occurs to me that I did not read many, if any, Australian writers in those days. But maybe that was the frustrated traveller in me – I was looking for wider horizons.

It is difficult to say what were the influences of my teenage days – you'll discover that when you reach your dotage: there's no eye so dreamy as the one that looks backwards. But to generalize, I'd say I was influenced by books that told me of a larger world than the one I could see from our front gate, by books that made me laugh, by books that told me a story and did not spend 200 pages asking me to contemplate the author's navel. Maybe, in the end, those latter books were the major influence – because that's what I eventually became myself: a story-teller.

H. C. "Nugget" Coombs

1906 – 1997

H.C. "Nugget" Coombs was born in Kalamunda, Western Australia, and educated at Perth Modern School where he remained as a pupil/teacher. He spent four years teaching while he studied at the University of Western Australia before proceeding to the London School of Economics where he completed a PhD in central banking. He returned to Australia in 1934 to become an economist with the Commonwealth Bank, joining the board in 1941. In 1942, he was appointed Director of Rationing and, in 1943, Director-General of the Department of Post-war Reconstruction. In 1960, when the Reserve Bank of Australia was created to take over the Commonwealth Bank's central banking functions, he was appointed Governor of the Reserve Bank. In 1967, he became chairman of the Council for Aboriginal Affairs. In 1972, he was named Australian of the Year. In 1976, he resigned all his posts and became a visiting fellow at the Centre for Resource and Environmental Studies at the Australian National University.

I doubt whether my experience is likely to prove elevating to your pupils' taste; my own is too discriminating. I early acquired an addiction to the printed word and since then have read everything that came my way. I have even been known to read the Hansard records of Parliamentary debates which should prove that my addiction is pathological.

As a child I was a regular subscriber to the *Magnet* and *Gem* school stories and to the *Boys' Own Paper*, as well as reading others like *Tom Brown's Schooldays* and even *Eric or Little by*

Little. I remember being especially pleased with the boys at Tom Brown's school getting the school magpie drunk on a diet of bread soaked in beer, which apparently was supplied for the boys' breakfast! Adventure stories by G.A. Henty and by Fenimore Cooper were important at this stage, but Mark Twain's *Tom Sawyer* and *Huckleberry Finn* were outstanding – particularly the latter which I still consider one of the really great books. Then followed a steady diet of 'Westerns' in magazines, paperbacks and a few more reputable books, like Zane Grey's *Riders of the Purple Sage*, which, I may say, now seems to me so dull that I wonder at any sensible teenager giving time to it.

The Count of Monte Cristo, The Man in the Iron Mask and other Dumas stories, Conan Doyle's Sherlock Holmes stories, some Robert Louis Stevenson and Kipling's *Kim, Tales from the Hills* and *Barrack Room Ballads* came in about this time and I recall being excited by some romantic tales of the English country side by somebody named Jeffrey Farnol of which I can now recall practically nothing.

My mother was an enthusiastic reader of 19th Century English novels, especially Dickens and I readily took to *Pickwick Papers, The Tale of Two Cities* and *David Copperfield*. I was less enthusiastic then about Thackeray and George Eliott, although I now rate the latter as one of the best English novelists. H.G. Wells, with both his pseudo-scientific stories and even more his social novels like *Kipps* and *Love and Mr Lewisham,* was a favourite at that time. It was only in my late teen years that I discovered Jane Austen whose novels have continued to delight me ever since.

In between all these I read whatever was at hand. In church to which my family took me regularly I whiled away the sermon time with the *Book of Common Prayer* and particularly the Table of Consanguinity (which, inter alia, forbade me to marry my Grandmother – a restriction on human liberty which enchanted me) and the ritual for the baptism of infants, from which I learned that my baby sister had come into the world possessed by evil spirits. I looked at her with new respect thereafter.

The Bible too, I found a mine of fascinating stories and of information frequently on topics about which my parents were somewhat unwilling to enlighten me. So too were the books my parents hid away from my curious eyes. I recall becoming goggle-eyed over a book they had hidden which described the goings-on of the Russian monk Rasputin with the noble ladies of the Czar's court. If all else failed I read the Dictionary.

I doubt whether these recollections are likely to inspire your students, or keep them away from the spurious delights of the 'Box', but perhaps they may persuade them that reading can be fun.

Sir Zelman Cowen

1919 - 2011

The Right Honourable Sir Zelman Cowen, AK, GCMG, GCVO, PC, was born in Melbourne and was educated at Scotch College and the University of Melbourne. He served in the RAN during World war II then attended New College, Oxford, as a Rhodes Scholar, remaining at Oxford as a Fellow of Oriel College from 1947 to 1950. In 1951 he was appointed Dean of the Law Faculty at the University of Melbourne and recognised as an expert in constitutional law. He served as Vice-Chancellor of the University of New England from 1966 to 1970 and the University of Queensland from 1970 to 1977. In 1977 he became Australia's 19th Governor-General. In 1982, he returned to Oxford as Provost of Oriel College. His published works include "Isaac Isaacs" (1962), "Sir John Latham" (1988) and "A Public Life – The Memoirs of Zelman Cowen" (2006).

From his Official Secretary:

The Governor-General turned 16 just as he left Scotch College (1935, Form VI). For most of his 5th Form year he was 14. He Would have entered his teens at the end of the year in Form III (Year 9).

In early teens the books that he read most avidly were the works of Dumas, particularly *The Count of Monte Cristo* and *The Three Musketeers*. He read current historical novel writing such as the books of Sabatini, which have now largely disappeared. He read in his early teens the English school classics like *Tom Brown's Schooldays* and others. Then he was greatly drawn to legal biography – the biographies of great English advocates. The special one was Edward Marjoribanks's *Life of Edward Marshall Hall*: that fuelled his ambition to become a practising barrister, though his life in the law took a rather different course.

In the Governor-General's latter teens, he read the Aldous Huxley books *Brave New World* and *Point Counterpoint* and the latter particularly made a great impression.

He read Sinclair Lewis's novels: he has a vivid memory at the end of his school days reading *It Can't Happen Here*, which had powerful point in those days of Hitler and Mussolini.

He read a great deal over those years, and these are some indications of what he read.

Finlay Crisp

1917 – 1984

Professor Finlay Crisp was born in Sandringham, Victoria, and educated at Black Rock State School, Caulfield Grammar School, St Peter's College, Adelaide, the University of Adelaide and Oxford University. He was a Rhodes Scholar for 1951. He worked for the Australian Public Service during World War II. In 1945, he was a member of the Australian Delegation to form the United Nations. He joined the Department of Labour and National Service, and became head of the Department of Post-War Reconstruction in 1949. From 1950, he was a professor of political science at the Canberra University College and then at the Australian National University, serving as head of the department from 1950 to 1970. He was appointed a director of the Commonwealth Banking Corporation in 1974, and served as chairman of the board from 1975 to 1984. His books include "Australian National Government", "Ben Chifley: A political Biography", "The Australian Federal Labour Party 1901-1951" and "Federation Fathers".

Thank you for your letter of June 9 on behalf of your Year 11 Class engaged on the interesting reading-matter project you have outlined to me.

My teens are a long way off now so it is not as easy as the class may think to recollect now, at once accurately and objectively, what book or books were my favourites or influenced me most in those days and why.

To be honest, it is now apparent to me, looking back, that what were my favourites and what influenced me most were sometimes two very different things. I spent much time, for instance, in enjoyment of English school stories in the books of Talbot Baines Reed or in serials in *The Magnet, The Gem, Chums* and *Boys' Own Paper.* They were favourites; but whether they had any positive or creative influence seems doubtful – unless to reinforce the Anglophile and Imperial attitudes my schools encouraged in those days.

To be objective, I was doubtless far from a typical boy (except in a widely-shared dislike of Maths!) for my favourite subjects were English, Greek, Latin, Ancient and British History – an almost vanished combination, even then. Those things have remained a joy and a recreation (though Greek plays and the Greek and Roman authors I read – lazily – in translation nowadays). In my later years at school, and afterwards, I moved increasingly to favourites amongst the fashionable writers in politics and economics.

As for books that influenced me in later years, it may sound pretentious but I should in all honesty have to list very high the King James translation of *The Bible* and the old Church of England *Book of Common Prayer* – not for any *religious* influence (I have been an agnostic from about 18) but because of their rich and marvellous English prose. At St Peter's in Adelaide we had daily chapel (and twice on Sundays) – without the option – and the constant exposure to the rhythm and construction of 17th century English (not to mention having to learn miles of Shakespeare and the English poets, as we had to do in those days) developed a fascination and a joy which have, if anything, grown over the years. Even thirty years of reading student essays and exam papers and theses, of steadily diminishing literary quality in many cases as the years have passed, have not blotted out the fascination with classical English prose and verse. Not, alas, that I write well even now, but it is something to have a measure and try to reach it.

You will have gathered I have always been something of a bookworm and am probably a stuffy old one now. If it does not sound too trite, however, I would give some comfort to those of the Year 11 class who have incipient tendencies in a similar direction – if you do develop tastes like those I have indicated above, the annual dividends of joy in them as the years go by seem to be increasingly worth the teenage toil and trouble.

This letter has got rather out of hand. Let the Year 11 have fun with an old gaffer's garrulity in their classroom where teachers of the past may have taught and whacked me long ago.

Paul Cronin

1938 – 2019

Paul Cronin was born in Jamestown, South Australia, and educated at Rostrevor College. He is well known for his leading roles in the television series "The Sullivans", "Matlock Police" and "Solo One". He won the Silver Logie five times and was one of the most popular actors working in the television industry in Australia.

During my primary education, the books I enjoyed reading consisted of mainly adventure stories. For example, B*iggles, Lassie*, etc.

During my secondary education, apart from the mandatory books set for study, I liked books that always seemed to be about persons or people who overcame handicaps of one kind or another. Allan Marshall's *I Can Jump Puddles* and Paul Brickhill's *Reach for the Sky* about war hero Douglas Bader are two examples.

I was greatly influenced by this type of book insofar as man's struggle to exist and overcome difficulties which were not only admirable but desirable.

Dymphna Cusack

1902 – 1981

Dymphna Cusack, AM, was born in Wyalong, New South Wales, and was educated at Saint Ursula's College, Armadale and the University of Sydney She worked as a teacher until she retired in 1944 for health reasons. She wrote twelve novels (two of which were collaborations), eleven plays, three travel books, two children's books and one non-fiction book. Her collaborative novels were 'Pioneers on Parade' (1939) with Miles Franklin, and 'Come In Spinner' (1951) with Florence James. The play 'Red Sky at Morning' was filmed in 1944, starring Peter Finch. The biography 'Caddie, the Story of a Barmaid', to which she wrote an introduction and helped the author write, was produced as the film 'Caddie' in 1976. The novel 'Come In Spinner' was produced as a television series by the Australian Broadcasting Corporation in 1989, and broadcast in March 1990. She advocated social reform and described the need for reform in her writings. She contributed to the world peace movement during the Cold War era as an antinuclear activist. She and her husband Norman Freehill were members of the Communist Party and they left their entire estates to the Party in their wills. She was a foundation member of the Australian Society of Authors in 1963. She was made a Member of the Order of Australia in 1981 for her contribution to Australian literature. In 2011, she was one of 11 authors, including Elizabeth Jolley and Manning Clark, to be permanently recognised by the addition of brass plaques at the Writers' Walk in Sydney.

I am delighted that you are interested in Australian writers – something not encouraged by the Academic Australian Literature Classes!

In answer to your question: When I was 13 or 14, growing sick of Ethel Turner, Mary Grant Bruce and my brother's CHUMS which were the favourite reading matter of the day, I wrote an essay for a competition in a magazine about my favourite book: a German circus story. It won the prize but evoked a letter from an old Irishman, Paddy Donovan. He praised my writing but said: "Why don't you read Australian books?" To encourage me, he sent me a second-hand copy of FOR THE TERM OF HIS NATUAL LIFE by Marcus Clarke. It enchanted me. Here was the terrible history of my own country told in a way that stirred all my dramatic feelings! Here was drama and tragedy at its highest. Here was the "underdog" the hero with whom I could sympathise with all my heart.

I think it was the beginning of my love for Australian History, which was very inadequately taught from Jose and Scott. It affected my writing at a time when little Australian material was taught – None at the University! My first three-act play, broadcast in 1938, stage-produced 3 years earlier (I helped pay for the electric light!) RED SKY AT MORNING had an Irish convict as its hero. Remember that was the day when the Irish were hardly human (1815). It was later published by Melbourne University Press.

Warmest regards and good reading to you and your Class.

John Cusack

1908 – 1980

John Cusack (who wrote as John Bede) was educated at Christian Brothers College in Waverley. By 1933, he was a manager at Electrolux and, when war broke out, he joined the RAAF. He was the author of two books about the war. "They Hosed Them Out" was originally published in 1965 and is a classic Australian war novel, inspired by the author's experiences as an air gunner. His second novel "You Can Only Die Once" was published in 1974.

John Cusack's widow, Catherine, sent the following letter in response to the boys' request:

Sorry to say my husband passed away in July. John wrote a very good war book that may interest you boys.

He was an air gunner stationed in England for four years & did 165 ops over Europe. So he was very lucky to come home safe & sound.

The book is written under John Bede (John's first two names). If you are interested & cannot get a copy from a library, I'll loan you a copy.

Sir James Darling

1899 - 1995

Sir James Darling, CMG, OBE, was born in Tonbridge, England, and was educated at Repton School. He served as a Second Lieutenant in the Royal Field Artillery in France and occupied Germany in 1918 and 1919 before reading history at Oriel College, Oxford. He taught from 1921 to 1924 at Merchant Taylors' School in Liverpool, before joining the staff of Charterhouse in Surrey. He was appointed as Headmaster of Geelong Grammar School in 1930 and remained in that post until 1961. Whilst at Geelong, he set up the Outward Bound campus, Timbertop, close to Mansfield and Mt Buller, where academic work was supplemented by a wide range of physical activity in accord with his educational philosophy of focusing less on achievement and more on learning. He encouraged selflessness and hard work over competitiveness and idleness. After his retirement as Headmaster he was, for several years, Chairman of the Australian Broadcasting Commission and wrote for newspapers, and published several books.

What things they do at schools now! Teenager covers a multitude of stages, but I suppose you mean about 14 – 16.

As a junior school boy I wallowed in G.A. Henty.

From him, in the prescribed limits the most important single book I read was Henty's *Rise of the Dutch Republic* but I soon graduated to the heroes of that pre-first-war period – Shaw – Wells – Chesterton – Belloc, and I suppose for entertainment rather than inspiration to Arnold Bennett and Galsworthy.

I think that possibly Galsworthy's plays *Strife – Justice* etc had some influence, but it is a long time ago and I read a great deal.

Motley was important because through him I learned to enjoy the reading of very long historical books and later enjoyed Froude, Macaulay, Gibbon and their like.

One of my favourite books was Charles Kingsley's *The Roman and the Teuton* but I am not sure when.

Sir Rohan Delacombe

1906 – 1991

An "honorary Australian" as he was Governor of Victoria from 1963 to 1974, Major-General Sir Rohan Delacombe, KCMG, KCVO, KBE, CB, DSO, KStJ, was born at St Julian's in Malta and educated in England at Harrow School and the Royal Military College, Sandhurst. Commissioned in the Royal Scots, he served in Palestine from 1937 to 1939 during the Arab revolt and went with the British Expeditionary Force to the Franco-Belgian border when Germany invaded Poland. During the Normandy campaign, he was awarded the Distinguished Service Order for his leadership during a sustained German counter-attack at Haut du Bosq in June, 1944. He was a General Staff Officer during the re-occupation of British Malaya from 1945 to 1947 and then spent much of the remainder of his career in Germany, becoming Commandant of the British Sector of Berlin in 1959. He retired from the army in 1962 before taking up his post as Governor of Victoria, the last British appointee to hold that post.

Sixty odd years ago boys of my age grew up in the days of Empire and the type of book we enjoyed was of another world and age.

However we enjoyed adventure stories which led us on to historical novels. For example the writings of John Buchan – *Castle Gay – The Thirty-Nine Steps – Huntingtower – Island of Sheep* and so to *Montrose*.

Books on the French Revolution such as *The Scarlet Pimpernel* by Baroness Orczy – The French Foreign Legion in *Beau Geste*

& Beau Sabreur.

The Riddle of the Sands by Erskine Childers but above all the works of Rudyard Kipling - Jungle Stories – poems of the days of the Raj in India. Books of the North West Frontier where, in later years, a lot of us served.

It was this type of book and story and its romance which guided us to follow the family tradition of service; a life which I enjoyed to the full in almost every part of the world.

Viscount De L'Isle, VC

1909 – 1991

Another "honorary Australian" as Governor-General of Australia from 1961 to 1965 was William Philip Sidney, VC, KG, GCMG, GCVO, KStJ, 1ˢᵗ Viscount De L'Isle who was born in London, educated at Eton College and Magdalene College, Cambridge, and became a chartered accountant. In 1929, he joined the Grenadier Guards Reserve of Officers. He served with the Grenadiers in Italy in World War II and was awarded the Victoria Cross for outstanding bravery during the defence of the Anzio beachhead in February 1944. Later that year, he was elected to the House of Commons but moved to the House of Lords in 1945 when he inherited his father's title of Baron De L'Isle and Dudley and served as Secretary of State for Air under Winston Churchill. He was created a Viscount in 1956.

One book I read as a "teenager" with interest and excitement was Basil Lubbock's *Round the Horn Before the Mast*.

It was a most stirring description of real people and real events against a background of the oceans.

The inspiration passed and I have since developed a positive distaste for the sea! But the book captured my youthful imagination and I can still recall the pleasure I felt when I read it.

Stuart Devlin

1931 – 2018

Stuart Devlin, AO, CMG, was born in Geelong and educated at the Gordon Institute of Technology before becoming an art teacher, specialising in gold and silversmithing. In 1957, he obtained a post at the Royal Melbourne Institute of Technology and studied for a Diploma of Art in gold and silversmithing. He was awarded scholarships to study at the Royal College of Art in London in 1958. He returned to teach in Melbourne and subsequently became an inspector of art schools. He rose to fame when, in 1964, he won a competition to design the first decimal coinage for Australia. In 1965, he moved to London and opened a workshop. He designed coins and medals for 36 countries throughout the world, including precious coins for the Sydney 2000 Olympic Games and the medals for the founding awards of the Australian honours system in 1975, the Order of Australia, the Australian bravery decorations and the National Medal.

Thank you for your letter of July 4th, although I am afraid my response will not help your cause.

My parents felt that reading was well down the scale of priorities, and that my time could be more profitably used in tasks requiring a greater personal contribution from me. The result was that I read virtually nothing other than what was compulsory at school.

In the light of the development of my career, who am I to say that reading is as important as educationalists tend to indicate.

Brian Dixon

Born 1936

The Honourable Brian Dixon was born in Melbourne and educated at Melbourne Boys' High School and the University of Melbourne. He became a teacher and, for a time, was head of the Economics Department at Melbourne Grammar School. He played 252 VFL games for the Melbourne Football Club between 1954 and 1968. He played in five premierships, winning Melbourne's best and fairest in 1960, while in 1961 he was selected in the All-Australian team. In 2000, he was named in Melbourne's Team of the Century. He entered parliament in 1964, as the member for the now abolished seat of St Kilda, representing the Liberal Party. He variously served in several portfolios including Youth, Sport and Recreation, Housing and Aboriginal Affairs. After leaving parliament in 1982, he worked predominantly in sports administration.

I am sorry that my reply is so short but my time is limited by circumstances beyond my control.

The book which influenced me most was the *New Testament* because it helped mould my value system and the book which was my favourite was Arthur Koestler's *Darkness at Noon* which taught me that ends don't justify means.

Rosemary Dobson

1920 – 2012

Rosemary Dobson, AO, was born in Sydney and attended Frensham School. She began writing poetry at the age of seven. She stayed on at Frensham, after completion of her studies, as an apprentice teacher of art and art history.

When she turned 21, she attended the University of Sydney as a non-degree student. She also studied design with Australian artist, Thea Proctor. She worked as an editor and reader for the publisher Angus and Robertson.

Her first collection of poetry, "In a Convex Mirror", appeared in 1944, and was followed by thirteen more volumes. Her work demonstrated her love of art, antiquity and mythology. She was also an illustrator, editor and anthologist.

Unfortunately I was away when your letter arrived, and now that has delayed my answer further. I'm so sorry. I hope my contribution may still be in time to be useful for your class project. However, it's very difficult to be specific about everything that came to hand in those formative years, and do not regret having done so now.

I read everything I could as a teenager. Early on I liked historical novels, or any which had strange or foreign settings.

I spent a great deal of time looking at books of Reproductions of Great Paintings of the World. These established a deep and lasting interest in art.

The poets whose work most influenced me at the time were, I should say – Shelley, Keats, Browning.

I should emphasise, however, that I read everything printed that came to hand.

Sir Edward "Weary" Dunlop

1907 – 1993

Sir Edward Dunlop, AC, CMG, OBE, was born in Wangaratta, Victoria, and was educated at Benalla High School. He started an apprenticeship in pharmacy and moved to Melbourne in 1927. There, he studied at the Victorian College of Pharmacy and then the University of Melbourne, where he obtained a scholarship in medicine. He graduated in 1934 with first class honours in pharmacy and in medicine, and excelled as a sportsman. At Ormond College, he took up rugby union. He rapidly progressed through the grades, to state, and then to the national representative level, becoming the first Victorian-born player to represent the Wallabies. In 1935 he was commissioned into the Australian Army Medical Corps. In May 1938 he left Australia for London. There he attended St Bartholomew's Medical School and became a Fellow of the Royal College of Surgeons. During the Second World War, he was appointed to medical headquarters in the Middle East, where he developed the mobile surgical unit. In Greece he liaised with forward medical units and Allied headquarters, and at Tobruk he was a surgeon until the Australian Divisions were withdrawn for home defence. His troopship was diverted to Java in an ill-planned attempt to bolster the defences there. He became a Japanese prisoner of war in 1942 when he was captured in Bandung, Java, together with the hospital he was commanding. Along with a number of other Commonwealth Medical Officers, his dedication and heroism became a legend among prisoners. A courageous leader and compassionate doctor, he restored morale in those terrible prison camps and jungle hospitals. Dunlop defied his captors, gave hope to the sick and eased the anguish of the dying. His example was one of the reasons why Australian survival rates were the highest. After 1945, with the darkness of the war years behind him, he forgave his captors and turned his energies to the task of healing and building. He was to state later that " in suffering we are all equal". He devoted himself to the health and welfare of former prisoners-of-war and their families, and worked to promote better relations between Australia and Asia.

As a country boy in days begore television, radio and cinema I red voraciously books of every sort. Also good literature – Shakespeare, Bunyan, Thackeray etc had less appeal than adventure stories: Kingsley *Westward Ho, Midshipman Easy*, R.M. Ballantine, *Coral Island*, R.L. Stevenson *Kidnapped, Treasure Island*, Fenimore Cooper, E.S. Ellis, Daniel Defoe (Robinson Crusoe) and particularly P.C. Wren, *Beau Geste,* etc which made us all candidates for the French Foreign Legion. Dumas *The Three Musketeers*. John Buchan with Richard Hannay's adventures *The Thirty-nine Steps, Greenmantle* etc came later – a remarkable discovery.

However to answer your main question I think Rider Haggard with the Alan Quartermain stories – *King Solomon's Mines, She*, etc had the most powerful grip on my imagination.

I eventually gave myself up to a future of short safaris, and fantastic peoples clouded in mystery.

The modern equivalent is my dear friend Laurens van der Post who worked closely with me in Java, and always sends me an autographed copy of the latest book – many of those African adventure stories in the atmosphere of the bright dawn of his boyhood.

Thank you for reminding me – many more old favourites keep surfacing, but I must stop. Best wishes for the project.

Dame Mary Durack

1913 – 1994

Dame Mary Durack, AC, DBE, was born in Adelaide and grew up on cattle stations in the Kimberley region of Western Australia. She began writing at an early age, publishing "Little Poems of Sunshine: By an Australian child" in 1923, a book of her poetry. Working with her sister Elizabeth as illustrator, she published a number of children's books, also writing for the Western Mail. Her books include "All About: The Story of a Black Community on Argyle Station, Kimberley" (1935), "The Way of the Whirlwind" (1941), "Keep Him My Country" (1955), "Kings in Grass Castles" (1959), "To Ride a Fine Horse" (1963), "The Aborigines in Australian Literature" (1978) and "Sons in the Saddle" (1983).

I cannot claim that I remember, as a teenager, any one book as having had more influence on me than any other.

From 6 to 10 or 11 years old I was attracted by the stories and pictures of May Gibbs and the Rentoul sisters.

Books that held my interest from about 10 years onwards were the novels of Ethel Turner and Mary Grant Bruce. Kipling (*Just So Stories, Jungle Stories, Kim,* etc.) was also favourite reading at this time.

From 12 years on I found the works of Charles Dickens, Walter Scott and Robert Louis Stevenson particularly absorbing. Dickens and Scott probably left the most lasting impression and awakened in me a keen sense of history and appreciation of social issues.

Having grown up before the age of radio and television programmes I must say that books were the greatest joy of my life and the characters that were part of them have remained as clear in my memory as living people.

Geoffrey Dutton

1922 - 1998

Geoffrey Dutton AO was a prodigious writer and editor whose published works comprise poetry, novels, children's books, biographies, art history and literary criticism. A native of South Australia, he was raised on his family's property Anlaby and educated at Geelong Grammar. While studying at the University of Adelaide he met Max Harris, co-founder of the literary magazine Angry Penguins, *and became a regular contributor to the magazine. Dutton joined the Royal Australian Air Force in 1941 and was a flying instructor, surviving a plane crash late in the war. His first collection of poetry, "Night Flight and Sunrise", was published in 1944. After the war, he studied English literature at Magdalen College, Oxford and lectured in English at Adelaide University. He and Harris founded the "Australian Book Review" in 1961 and later Dutton founded the publishing house Sun Books. He published many collections of poetry, including "Antipodes in Shoes" in 1958. His autobiography "Out in the Open", was published in 1994.*

My favourite books as a teenager were very much a mixed bag, and fall into two divisions, for my tastes changed abruptly after 1938-39. (I was born in 1922).

In my early teens my favourite books were *The Iliad* and *The Odyssey, Myths and Legends of Ancient Greece and Rome*, and *Norse Myths and Legends.* When I was young I had almost no children's books, but my mother read me these, and later I read them myself avidly. I was besotted about two books by Ernest

Thompson Seton, who sometimes called himself Ernest Seton Thompson, *Lives of the Hunted* and *Wild Animals I Have Known*. All these books gave me a taste for heroes and courage and skill and far-off places.

No doubt this taste also explains a rather lowlier passion for the works of "Sapper", Leslie Charteris and Ion L. Idriess, all of which I devoured entire; likewise Rider Haggard. There was something indefinably sexy about *Ayesha* and *She*, likewise the dreadful Jeffery Farnol whom I nevertheless read entire!

About 1938 poetry became my favourite reading, especially W.H. Auden, Spender and *The Faber Book of Modern Verse* which appeared a bit later.

In the first section I see I've left out *Robbery Under Arms*, *For The Term of His Natural Life* and *Geoffrey Hamlyn*, the only Australian books, apart from Idriess, I ever read.

Good luck with your project. With me it is rather a case of the biter bit, as a couple of months ago I sent out a circular to about 60 Australian writers over 30, asking them what Australian books they had read in their childhood and teens. The startling results I'm writing up for *The Bulletin*.

Sir Hughie Edwards, VC

1914 – 1982

Air Commodore Sir Hughie Edwards, VC, KCMG, CB, DSO, OBE, DFC, was born in Fremantle, Western Australia and was educated at White Gum Valley School and Fremantle Boys' High School. Leaving school at 14, he worked in a horse racing stable in Fremantle before joining the army in 1934 but, in 1935, was selected for flying training in the RAAF and then transferred to the RAF in 1936. Surviving a flying accident, he flew Blenheim bombers. In 1941, he became CO of 105 Squadron and led raids over Germany, in one of which his Blenheim was hit over 20 times but he completed his mission, flying at a low level. His outstanding bravery was recognised by the award of the Victoria Cross. He had previously been awarded the Distinguished Flying Cross and later would receive the Distinguished Service Order, for bravery and leadership in the face of the enemy. With the end of the European campaigns in sight, he was transferred to the Pacific theatre. In January 1945, he was appointed the senior administrative staff officer at Headquarters, South East Asia Command; serving in this position until the conclusion of the war. He continued his career in the RAF after the war; retiring in 1963 with the rank of air commodore. Returning to Australia, he became Governor of Western Australia from 1974 to 1975.

Thank you for your letter dated 24th June. I regret that I do not think you will consider me an ideal reader for your admirable project. In my teens I do not think I had any favourite books or any that influenced me greatly.

Of course, I read *Tom Sawyer, Huckleberry Finn, Last of the Mohicans, The Deerslayer*, etc. etc. and all the other potboilers for youth. I was fascinated by the first half of a book called *Northwest Passage*, by Kenneth somebody.* It was in two segments; I thought the second part tailed off.

I read a lot of poetry and was and still am an avid fan of Longfellow & Macaulay.

I must also confess I was a glutton for those English school weeklies like the *Gem* and the *Magnet*. Although not educational, to an Australian schoolboy they were most interesting & extended one's vocabulary.

You may be amused to know that when I was aged 9 at a primary school in West Australia we were re-stacking the library and pupils were asked for a suggestion. Being smart & precocious I suggested *Pickwick Papers*. Needless to say I had to wade through both copies. In 1974 I revisited the school, recounted the story to the headmaster. He replied that since I returned to books in 1924, they had never left the library.

*[The author of *Northwest Passage* was Kenneth Roberts]

Tony Eggleton

1932 – 2023

Tony Eggleton, AO, CVO, was born in the United Kingdom and educated at King Alfred's College in Berkshire. He was a cub reporter on his hometown paper in Swindon, Wiltshire, when, in 1950, he was invited to undertake work experience with the "Bendigo Advertiser" in Australia. He later joined the Australian Broadcasting Commission and played a role in the introduction of television in Australia in 1956. in 1970 he played a leading role in organising the tour of Australia by Queen Elizabeth II. In 1971, he was appointed Director of Information at the Commonwealth Secretariat in London. In 1974 he returned to Australia when Malcolm Fraser appointed him as his chief of staff and this led to his appointment as Federal Director of the Liberal Party, a post he held for 15 years. In 1991 he was appointed secretary-general of CARE International, one of the world's largest private international humanitarian organisations. In 1997 the government appointed him Chief Executive of Australia's programme to celebrate the Centenary of Federation in 2001.

Thank you for your letter of 24 June about the reading project at your school.

In my teens, it was books that extended my horizons and stimulated my ambitions. In the English factory town in which I grew up, I read just about anything that I could get from the local library – with a special interest in books about journalism and travel.

But perhaps the small volume that I remember best was, in fact, a school text book. It was a selection of poetry called *Verse Worth Remembering*. It contained a poem with sentiments that might be regarded as a little old fashioned these days:-

If you can keep your head when all about you

Are losing theirs and blaming it on you;

If you can trust yourself when all men doubt you,

But make allowance for their doubting too; . . .

If you can fill the unforgiving minute

With sixty seconds worth of distance run,

Yours is the Earth and everything that's in it,

And – what is more – you'll be a Man, my son!

Extracts, of course, from Rudyard Kipling's *If*. That ancient text book of early 1940 vintage still sits on my book-shelves in Canberra. I am indebted to *Verse Worth Remembering*.

Good luck with your project.

Herb Elliott

Born 1938

Herb Elliott, AC, MBE, was born in Perth, Western Australia and educated at Aquinas College where he was Head Prefect in the Class of 1955. He later attended the University of Cambridge. In August 1958 he set the world record in the mile run; later in the month he set the 1500 metres world record. In the 1500 metres at the 1960 Rome Olympics, he won the gold medal and bettered his own world record. Elliott retired from athletics soon after the 1960 Olympics, at the age of 22. He made a career in business, and at one time was chairman of Fortescue Metals Group. He was also chairman of Global Corporate Challenge health initiative.

Thankyou for your letter of May 22nd. I find the challenge which you issue to delve back into my memory for many many years rather embarrassing. The latter years of my teenage life were the years in which I dedicated myself to personal improvement in the athletic world and during that time I had close contact with a very widely read and knowledgeable gentleman called Percy Cerutty. Percy was an avid reader and by this means became a highly self educated gentleman. His reading covered the field of Politics, the Arts, Psychology, Religion including of course *The Bible* and matters relating to physical education. During the years which I shared with Percy Cerutty, I read many of these books and they together with the inspiration of Cerutty himself led me to believe that if I really wanted a goal badly enough, I would be able to achieve it.

I also remember struggling my way through one or two deeply philosophical books which I only half understood. I can however, not remember the name of a single title. I don't know whether this means that each book I read influenced me equally, none influenced me at all (and I know this not to be true) or I have just got a bad memory. I think it may be the latter.

I therefore beg the forgiveness of your Year 11 English Class for not being able to answer the question. However, I can emphatically say that the reading which I did do played an important part in my self development and was all the more stimulating because the normal sequence was to read the book and then become involved in active discussion with Percy Cerutty and other members of our group who used to train together on the subject matter of the book. This brought the ideas of the author to life in our own minds and assisted us to arrive at our own conclusions.

I wish you the best of luck with your project and hope that you obtain more detailed answers from others that you have written to. Best wishes.

Sumner Locke Elliott

1917 – 1991

With his father overseas and his mother dying the day after he was born, Sumner Locke Elliott was brought up by a clowder of aunts who moved him between their homes. He eventually attended Cranbrook as a boarder for his primary education then completed the Intermediate Certificate at Neutral Bay High School. He wrote and produced plays whilst still at school then worked for J.C. Williamson Ltd and in radio. Seven of his plays were produced in Sydney between 1937 and 1948. He served full-time in the Citizen Military Forces from 1942 to 1946 then Moved to New York in 1949, becoming a leading scriptwriter. He wrote ten ovels including "Careful He Might Hear You" (1963), "Water Under the Bridge" (1977), "Waiting for Childhood" (1987) and "Fairyland" (1990). He became an American citizen in 1955.

In my public high school days literature was to be avoided like scabies. Possibly because in those days the standard book set was conventional nineteenth century literature such as *Ivanhoe, Quentin Durward* and *The White Company,* all of which we struggled through.

In my personal time in my early teens I discovered *The Scarlet Pimpernel* by Baroness Orczy third rate literature but astonishingly vivid picture of the French Revolution and led me to *Tale of Two Cities, David Copperfield, Pickwick Papers, Les Miserables,* Sherlock Holmes, *Silas Marner.* I think my first dynamic reaction to a novel was *Wuthering Heights.* For all its passion and beauty it was considered too evocative for young boys then. I also relished *Huckleberry Finn* and *We the Living* by Ayn Rand.

Noel Ferrier

1930 – 1997

Noel Ferrier, AM, was born in Melbourne. A member of the first Australian professional repertory company, the Union Theatre Repertory Company (now the Melbourne Theatre Company), he created the role of "Roo" in the original production of "Summer of the Seventeenth Doll" at the Union Theatre. He appeared in numerous films and television productions. A contemporary of Barry Humphries, in 1956 he was the "interviewer" of the first onstage appearance of a certain Mrs. Norm Everage, later known universally as Dame Edna Everage.

He appeared in such television series as "Riptide", "Skippy", "Homicide", "Division 4" and "Matlock Police". In 1982, he set up the musical theatre arm of the Elizabethan Theatre Trust. For Sydney Theatre Company he appeared in the original productions of David Williamson's "Sons of Cain" and "The Perfectionist"". In 1988, he became Artistic Director of the Marian Street Theatre.

His movie credits include "Avengers of the Reef", "Alvin Purple", "Alvin Rides Again", "Scobie Malone", "Deathcheaters", "Eliza Fraser", "Turkey Shoot", "The Year of Living Dangerously", "Backstage" and "Paradise Road".

I read with great interest your letter of 24th June 1980 concerning the type of reading which boys at your school may adopt to increase their proficiency.

Thank you for letting me off 'a long essay' and I shall just simply say –

> S.J. Perelman
> P.G. Wodehouse
> Alexander Woolcott
> Robert Benchley
> and the plays of Sheridan
> etc. etc. etc..

Thank you for including me and good luck with your project.

Joan Fitzhardinge

1912– 2003

Joan Fitzhardinge, AM, was a renowned children's author and published 31 books, all but two being fiction. She was born in Warrawee in New South Wales and educated at Frensham School. Much of her life growing up was spent travelling between Australia and England, visiting her English family. She studied journalism and worked for Reuters before World War II. During the war, she served as a telegraphist in the Women's Australian Auxiliary Air Force. Publishing her first novel in 1953, she went on to win a series of awards for children's books in Australia and the USA. She is perhaps best known for writing "Good Luck to the Rider", "The Family Conspiracy" and "The Watcher in the Garden".

Telling people your favourite books is rather like giving away your closest secrets. I would like to be able to list all the very best children's classics, graduating to the best of adult classics as my favourite reading. But I would be lost at the start by having to admit that I could never like Hans Andersen. But I don't suppose anyone else could, in honesty, do much better. The Perfect Reader hasn't been born yet.

When I was eleven I was still reading animal stories. I liked these best of all and read nothing else for some years. My favourite authors were Ernest Thompson Seton and Charles G.D. Roberts, both, I think, Canadians. I also loved Jack London's *White Fang* and *The Call of the Wild*. I liked exciting stories and I liked stories with as few people in them as possible. Then, as I grew older I began to read romantic, sentimental stories like *The Scarlet*

Pimpernel, Beau Geste, Tell England and Vachell's *The Hill* – all I would guess, very much dated now and very much stories for girls. But I also liked Dumas, *The Three Musketeers* and *The Count of Monte Cristo.* Together with these, urged by my teachers, I began to read Robert Louis Stevenson's *Kidnapped, Catriona* and *The Master of Ballantrae.* I needed no urging to read the Brontes, and *Jane Eyre* and *Wuthering Heights* were books I read over and over again. Then I made the acquaintance of Thomas Hardy and (so sheltered were we in those days) felt quite wicked to be reading *Tess of the d'Urbevilles.*

As I write this I can see a strand developing that begins to explain why I write now mainly about country matters, the open air, and, frequently, animals. Those well-loved animal books, those adventure stories, the Brontes, Thomas Hardy – they all, I think, point to a way of thinking and a way of life that leads out under the sky and relates to natural things.

The big question is: are my tendencies as a writer in this general direction because of the books I've read, or have these particular books been my favourites because this is the way I am, and this is the way I would have written anyway?

Perhaps the boys of your school can tell me?

Malcolm Fraser

1930-2015

The Right Honourable Malcolm Fraser, AC, CH, PC, was born in Toorak into a family of pastoralists and politicians. He attended Melbourne Grammar School and later graduated from the University of Oxford. He entered the Australian Parliament in 1955 as the Member for Wannon, holding the seat for 28 years. He served as Minister for the Army and later as Minister for Defence and became Prime Minister in 1975 following the dismissal of the Whitlam government. He resigned from parliament after his government lost the election in 1983. He helped bring an end to apartheid in South Africa as co-Chairman of the Commonwealth Committee of Eminent Persons. He published "Common Ground: Issues that Should Bind and Not Divide Us" in 2002, "Malcolm Fraser: The Political Memoirs" in 2010 and "Dangerous Allies" in 2014.

Naturally I enjoyed certain books at different ages and stages but two of my favourite authors during my early school years were Arthur Ransome and George Henty.

I particularly enjoyed the lively stories of sailing, adventure and nature lore by Mr Ransome. His works such as *Swallows and Amazons* were expressive and full of vigour, promoting adventure, spirit and perhaps above all positive thinking. They were very much in-tune with the twentieth century. Similarly Mr Henty's historical novels set in India and Africa were very popular for much the same reasons.

I should also add that another favourite book at this time was Rolph Boldrewood's *Robbery Under Arms.*

I wish you and your class every success with the project, and trust I have not 'missed the boat'.

Frank Galbally

1922 – 2005

One of the first solicitors to practise as a trial advocate without joining the Victorian Bar, Frank Galbally, CBE, was largely a criminal defence lawyer. He was born in Melbourne and educated at St Patrick's College, East Melbourne, leaving school at 16 to train for the priesthood. When Pearl Harbour was bombed, he joined the navy but did not go abroad. He played football for Collingwood in the 1942 season but a wood-chopping injury ended his football career. He was admitted to the University of Melbourne where he graduated with a Bachelor of Laws degree. Aside from his highly successful legal career, he served as Chairman of the Australian Institute of Multicultural Affairs and was decorated several times by the Italian government for his service to the Italian community in Australia. In 1982, he published, with Robert Macklin, "Juryman", in 1983 "Galbally for the Defence" and in 1989 "Galbally! The Autobiography of Australia's Leading Criminal Lawyer".

The books which influenced me most as a teenager were generally those of fictional adventure, historical adventure and biographical works dealing with persons who had sacrificed their lives for a cause. I list the following examples:

Captains Courageous

All Quiet on the Western Front

Beau Geste

The Diary of Willy Doyle (a Jesuit Priest who worked as a Chaplain in the 1914-1918 War in the trenches, and whose life was one of sacrifice.)

Belinda of the Red Cross (the saga of a nurse during the 1914-1918 War, looking after the wounded.)

Ken G. Hall

1901 – 1994

Kenneth George Hall, AO, OBE, was born in Paddington and was educated at North Sydney Boys' High School. At the age of 17, he became a publicist for Union Theatres. He had a six-month stint as manager for the Lyceum Theatre then returned to publicity, working his way up to national publicity director, the highest post in film publicity in Australia at that time.

In 1924, he joined the American distribution company First National Pictures as a publicist, and visited Hollywood the following year.

He began making films in 1928 when at First National he was assigned to recut and shoot additional sequences for a German movie about the Battle of Cocos, "Our Emden".

He eventually became assistant to Stuart F. Doyle, managing director of the company. Doyle established Cinesound Productions to make local films and assigned Hall to direct a number of shorts. Hall persuaded Bert Bailey to make a film of "Dad and Dave" and the result was a massively popular film, which was among the top four most popular films in Australian cinemas in 1932, earning £46,000 in Australia and New Zealand by the end of 1933.

After a stint in Hollywood, Hall returned to Australia with new filmmaking equipment and an American, who was to take over Cinesound's story department. His most notable newsreel was the Oscar-winning "Kokoda Front Line" in 1942 – the first time an Australian film/

documentary was awarded an Oscar.

After the war Hall returned to feature film production, enjoying a big success with "Smithy", a film biography of Australia's most famous aviator, Sir Charles Kingsford Smith, which he produced, co-wrote and directed.

HIs short subjects included "Can John Braund Cure Cancer? " in 1948, "Fighting Blood" in 1951, and "Overland Adventure" in 1956.

In 1956, Hall became the first general manager for Channel Nine in Sydney, where he remained until 1966. There he instigated the practice of showing feature films uncut; previously in Australia they had been cut to fit the television schedules.

Stage 3 at Fox Studios in Sydney was named after him.

I was delighted to receive your letter and even more delighted to learn that boys are still interested in reading.

When I was young, a long time ago – prior to my teens – I was an avid reader. My family has told me that I bemoaned the fact that I could not read (at about five I guess) to the point of occasional tears. Then when the magic of reading was sufficiently revealed to me – at about seven I suppose but cannot be sure at this great distance – I read everything in sight. Like a glutton, two or three books at a time, jumping from one to the other; but never cheating by jumping to the end of any of them to find out what happened – without absorbing why it happened.

And the books? Well they may not appeal to the youth of today because tastes change. Basically I feel that boys of this era are the same kind of boys I knew in the very early years of the century and, if the moderns can tear themselves away from television for a while, they may turn to reading and seek adventure stories as I did. When I first became really conscious of the great big world around me – and the marvels that lay between the Main in the company of *Mr Midshipman Easy*, with Charles Kingsley who sent me sailing *Westward Ho!* and again with *Eastward Ho!* with Captain Marryat (if that is the correct spelling of his name) and other writers who took their inspiration from history and, in fiction, brought it vividly to life for me. Rafael Sabatini, that more adult swashbuckler, took over later.

Then Fenimore Cooper, the splendid American creator of *The Deerslayer, The Last of the Mohicans*; wonderful stories. Most, if not all of them, revealed intimate knowledge of that great – and much maligned – race, the American Indian. Later I gratefully remember reading Scott and the Waverley novels and *Ivanhoe* in particular. I read and enjoyed Jules Verne who was considered to be altogether too way out by many of his time and later. But events have proved that his vivid imagination was not way out at all.

Mark Twain, that fabulous story teller, loomed over my horizon with *Tom Sawyer*, *Huckleberry Finn* and all the rest. I am sure I do not have to tell you of perhaps the greatest story teller of them all, Charles Dickens because he, with Thackeray would, I feel, still be prescribed reading in most good schools. I liked much of what Conan Doyle wrote, as did of course, millions of others.

Today young minds seem to be largely on space and I do not quarrel with that. Space, marvellous to contemplate, is obviously the future. From here to Infinity – or should that be Eternity? It has been there for billions of years. Perhaps it has always been there. Why should it end? Merely because everything in our existence begins and ends and that one fact influences all our judgements of all things?

My quarrel is with what the science fiction writers and Hollywood – and particularly Hollywood! – are doing to outer space. Oh I respect the brilliance of the movie world's designers and the marvellous craftsmanship of the Special Effects technicians who make films like *Star Wars* a dazzling experience for you. But not for me. I must confess I don't go to see them. I get bored. Because, having been a filmmaker so long, here and overseas, I can see the lath and plaster sets, past the models or miniatures and through the trick photography to know the phoneyness of it all. They have just taken the Goodies and the Baddies off the Praries and tossed them into the sky, without their six-guns but with far more deadly armour. I hope that Space is not like their version. But hope it is not good enough – I am SURE it is not.

I can believe there are other inhabitants of space besides ourselves – why should we have all the privileges? And why again must our films and our fiction take war to them? The oldest and by far the worst invention of mankind?

Someday, when space is more widely explored, as assuredly will be, we may contact people or beings from an advanced civilization, older and far superior mentalities, and leaders, to the best we have in this world. A race that will teach us how to live and not to die. A society in which there is no greed or avarice, no viciousness, no trace of man's inhumanity to man. Where there is no rich and no poor. A preachment you think? Wrong, because I am not a religious man. Utopian then? Perhaps, but is there anything wrong with Utopia? – other than we are going the wrong way about trying to realize it.

Perhaps, boys, what I am really trying to say to you is – try taking your heads out of the clouds and getting your feet firmly on the ground again. Pass up the flashy, completely unreal trash being served to you in films and paperbacks (e.g. *Star Wars* and its coming sequel *The Empire Strikes Back* which have made, and will continue to make, fortunes for some people in Hollywood but will do nothing for your minds) and get back to reality and truth of literature, old and new. I think you will find joy in it as I did.

Thank you for the challenge and I am sorry I ran over length somewhat but you see I like to read and write. With best wishes for the project.

Rodney Hall

Born 1935

Author of some 12 novels, 15 volumes of poetry and eight anthologies, Rodney Hall, AM, was born in England and came to Australia after World War II as a child. He was educated at the City of Bath Boys' School, Brisbane Boys' College and the University of Queensland where he graduated with a Bachelor of Arts degree. He worked variously as a scriptwriter, actor, film critic and music teacher, was editor of "Overland" magazine and poetry editor for "The Australian" newspaper. Literary prizes came his way including the Grace Leven Prize, the Miles Franklin Award (twice) and the Victorian Premier's Literary Award. He was Chair of the Australia Council from 1991 to 1994.

It's very difficult to be accurate about this. The books I now remember as having been influential are, I suppose, the ones which I know I enjoyed then and which I still do enjoy (for this reason I remember them, whereas many books I read and loved at the time I have now forgotten about altogether). So my list looks rather sophisticated. In fact, I wasn't a great reader at all. And until I had to read lots of books in a short time for university exams, at the age of 30, I was a very slow reader, taking weeks and even months over a single book. I'm still the slowest reader among my literary friends: but I read very exactly and carefully. And these days I read only masterpieces. If I start a book and it turns out not to be a masterpiece, I won't waste my time finishing it. This is a great plan, because for most of my life I finished books religiously, even when I hated them and they stopped me reading anything else for months at a time.

So to my list. The ages are reasonably accurate, because we moved about a lot and lived in different places and I associate books with various specific places, towns, schools, rivers, houses, and so on.

> age: 13 *Dusty* by Frank Dalby Davison and *Swallows & Amazons* by Arthur Ransome
>
> 14 *The Flight of the Heron* (the author's name I can't recall) * and *Treasure Island* by Robert Louis Stevenson
>
> 15 *Great Expectations* by Charles Dickens and *Here's Luck* by Lennie Lower
>
> 16 *Candide* by Voltaire and *Arms & The Man* by George Bernard Shaw (this was the year I left school, as my change in reading might indicate)
>
> 17 *Gargantua and Pantagruel* by Rabelais and *The Grapes of Wrath* by John Steinbeck
>
> 18 *Scarlet and Black* by Stendahl and *The Moon and Sixpence* by Somerset Maugham
>
> 19 *Pride and Prejudice* by Jane Austen, *Short Stories* by Henry Lawson, Guy de Maupassant and Rudyard Kipling, *Such is Life* by Tom Collins. Also *Selected Verse* by John Manifold

I hope this answers your question adequately. Up to the age of 16 I was more interested in paintings than books, and after 16 I got very involved with music. So my influences should really include Goya, Velasquez, Giotto, Botticelli, Turner, Cezanne, Mozart, Purcell, Berlioz, Schubert and Debussy as well. Also the Elizabethan songwriters.

*[*The Flight of the Heron* was written by D.K. Broster]

Dame Joan Hammond

1912 – 1996

Born in Christchurch, New Zealand, Dame Joan Hammond, DBE, CMG, was educated at Presbyterian Ladies' College at Pymble and won many titles in golf and swimming. In 1933, she was runner-up in the Australian amateur golf title.

She studied music at the Sydney Conservatorium, initially as a violinist, and singing in Vienna, making her operatic debut there in 1936. She sang in the great opera houses of the world and was renowned for her portrayal of Puccini's heroines. Her recording of Puccini's "O, my beloved father" sold over a million copies. She retired in 1965 and taught singing at the Victorian College of the Arts.

I consider myself very fortunate that I was born with a love of poetry, history and epic tales, also Greek and Roman mythology. My love of myths was fired by a specific teacher. At the age of thirteen, this excellent teacher would give us a lesson every week with slides. These photos of Athens and Rome and the beautiful works of art connected with myths, showed us such scenes as the Resting Hermes, a Greek bronze found at Herculaneum and now at the National Museum, Naples. We saw Velasquez' Bacchus at the Forge of Hephaestus; the lovely Pan and Psyche of Sir E. Burne-Jones; Watts Endymion; Lord Leighton's Herakles' Struggle with Death for the life of Alcestis and a myriad other incomparable works of art such as the Mourning Penelope at the Vatican.

I did not fully imbibe the enormity of the subject during my "teens" but I certainly have since. When I first studied the opera

Dido and Aeneas my mind went back to those lectures with slides and I was able to picture immediately the plot and source from which Purcell and his librettist gathered the material for the opera. Books on myths have always been part of my reading life.

My innate love of poetry developed rapidly during those vital years between twelve and twenty. My singing teacher have me "Where the bee sucks", "She never told her love" "When icicles hang by the wall" and many other songs set to Shakespearian words. When looking up the plays, from which the words were taken, became a marvellous type of game for me. *The Tempest, Twelfth Night* and *Love's Labour Lost* led me to the sonnets which, at the time, were outside the plays such as *Hamlet, King John, Merchant of Venice* etc given me to study.

Each term, an act, or complete work of a Shakespeare play was put on and this made them come to life when I was given a part to act. It whetted my appetite for more.

It was at this time that I was told to learn by heart and recite *The Highwayman* by Alfred Noyes. This poem had a profound effect on me. It stirred the romantic images and a greater love and understanding of colourful words. Such lines as "The wind was a torrent of darkness among the gusty trees..." "The moon was a ghostly galleon tossed upon cloudy seas..." "The road was a ribbon of moonlight over the purple moor..." There is also a feeling of urgency as the Highwayman comes "riding up to the old inn door" – not perhaps great, but, stirring words which rolled off the tongue.

These early introductions into the world of poetry have caused me during my career to study the poets of many other countries.

Music and poetry are synonymous, so at that early age, I was loving the poems through music. Ben Jonson's *Drink to me Only* led me to Donne, Tennyson, Rosetti, De La Mare, Masefield, Burns, Shelley, Keats, Browning, Wordsworth, Herrick, Masefield and so on, down the ages to our modern poets. It has been, and remains, an exhilarating, exciting journey built on words.

A for the books read, and re-read during these formative years of the "teens" which impressed me and left indelible marks, to name but a few, beginning with Kipling's *Jungle Stories*, which I was given earlier in life but which I continued to enjoy throughout my teens. Then came a craze for any Baroness Orczy book – *The Scarlet Pimpernel* – and others. This author made me want to visit Paris. Also, at this time, I developed a passion for Jeffrey Farnol novels. These made me long to be in England!

It was truly a romantic period for me, and then, at about sixteen my taste took a serious turn. I read, and cried, over most of Charles Dickens, Tolstoy and Dostoyevski. I relished Victor Hugo, Conrad, Thackeray, Verne, H.G. Wells, Trollope, Conan Doyle, Wilkie Collins – all of which taught me a great deal about the modes and manners of their time. There was good and evil in these stories, and society of that era was presented in such an interesting, naturalistic manner. One became caught up with a number of individuals, and the descriptions of their lives and manners influenced me in my behaviour at that time.

Soon after that spate of reading, I became enmeshed in the Bronte sisters and their writing. *Wuthering Heights* gripped me, so much so that I could not put it down. At the age of nineteen, I was given a copy of *The Wind in the Willows* by Kenneth Grahame. This delightful book was first published in the early twentieth century. My taste, as you can see, hovered about the mid-nineteenth century to the early twenties.

There is one book that has had a continuous effect on me throughout my entire life – *The Bible*. The interest in *The Bible* was kindled by my learning to sing extracts from the *The Messiah* and *Elijah* at the age of eighteen. It was after this that I began to enjoy reading certain books such as Luke and the Acts, Ruth, Joseph, David, John the Baptist, Esther, Judas Maccabaeus and many more. The Bible is an extraordinary book, because no matter how often you pick it up, there is always some grain of knowledge to be found on any page which you have previously read and missed.

Lang Hancock

1909 – 1992

Lang Hancock was born in Leederville, Western Australia. He was initially educated at home then, at the age of eight, he began boarding at the St Aloysius Convent of Mercy in Toodyay. He later attended Hale School in Perth. Upon completing his secondary education, he returned to Mulga Downs Station to help his father manage the property. During the Second World War, he served in a militia unit, the 11th (North-West) Battalion, Volunteer Defence Corps. On 16 November 1952, Hancock claimed he discovered the world's largest deposit of iron ore in the Pilbara region of Western Australia. Famous for this discovery, he became one of the richest men in Australia. In the mid-sixties, he and his partner entered into a deal with mining giant Rio Tinto Group to develop the iron ore find. Under the terms of the deal, Rio Tinto set up and still administer a mine in the area.

Thank you for your letter of 24th June.

It's been a long time since I was a teenager, however, the books that I found worthwhile are:-

The 1904 W.A. *Mining Act* – which gave security of tenure and thus allowed the development of W.A.'s mining industry – until supplementary legislation passed, taking away security of tenure and prohibiting right to appeal in Court which is unique in Westminster system.

Ayn Rand – *Atlas Shrugged* and other books. This points out the tragedy of excessive government.

And more recently, Milton Friedman's *There's no Such Thing as a Free Lunch*, and other books, which should be read in every school.

W.K. Hancock

1898 – 1988

Sir William Hancock, KBE, FBA was born in Melbourne and educated at Melbourne Grammar School and the University of Melbourne. As the Rhodes Scholar for 1921, he studied at Balliol College, Oxford. He graduated in 1924 with a Bachelor of Arts with first class honours in Modern History. He was Professor of Modern History at the University of Adelaide between 1924 and 1933 and at the University of Adelaide between 1924 and 1933. Between 1944 and 1949, he returned to Oxford, becoming Professor of Economic History. In 1949 he left Oxford, taking up an appointment as the Director of the Institute of Commonwealth Studies. He served as the Professor of British Commonwealth Affairs at the University of London until 1956. Hancock returned to Australia in 1957 to take up an appointment as Director of the Research School of Social Sciences at the Australian National University, a position he held until 1961. He was Professor of History at the Institute of Advanced Studies, ANU until his retirement in 1965.

In reply to your letter of 4 July –

Of the many books which I read with profit and delight during my schooldays, I return most often to:

Plato, *The Apology of Socrates, Crito*

Shakespeare, *King Lear*

Wordsworth, *The Prelude*

Old Testament, Job

Dickens, *Great Expectations*

Rolf Boldrewood, *Robbery Under Arms*

Pro Hart

1928 – 2006

Kevin Charles "Pro" Hart, MBE, was born in Broken Hill and grew up on his family's sheep farm in Menindee. He was educated at the Marist Brothers College and the Broken Hill Technical College. He was nicknamed "Professor" (hence "Pro") during his younger days, when he was known as an inventor. Hart typically painted with oils or acrylics, using paint brushes and sponges, and depict scenes of rural town life, nature, topical commentary, and some religious subject. His illustrations for the collection of Henry Lawson's poems show keen powers of character observation combined with an obvious wit. Hart was also a sculptor, working with welded steel, bronze and ceramics. He received an Australian Citizen of the Year award in 1983.

From his secretary: Mr Hart has been away quite a lot and we have become behind in our mail.

Pro's favourites have always been the poems of Banjo Patterson and Henry Lawson and the story of Waltzing Matilda. You can see this in the books of Poems he has illustrated i.e. *Poems of Henry Lawson* Vol. 1 & 2, *Poems of Banjo Paterson* Vol. 1 & 2, *Bush Ballads* and *Waltzing Matilda* which recently came out. His next book he will be illustrating will be on Breaker Morant. He also is very interested in Australian History, Bush Rangers and the old Coaching days e.g. his Cobb. & Co. series.

Pro Hart is just a true lover of Australia and paints it as he sees it.

Many thanks for your letter.

Sir Lawrence Hartnett

1898 - 1986

*Sir Laurence Hartnett, CBE, was born in Woking, Surrey,
in England and educated at Kingston Grammar School
and Epsom College. He served with the Royal Navy
and Royal Air Force before becoming head of General
Motors' English subsidiary, Vauxhall. In 1934, General
Motors acquired the Australian company established
by Sir Edward Holden in 1917, and Hartnett took up
the position of Managing Director of General Motors
Holden, Australia, with the brief to either boost profits
or shut the operation down. Profits were boosted, thanks
to his management skills. He was also Director of the
Commonwealth Aircraft Corporation from 1935 to
1947. When the war ended, the Australian government
was keen to produce a local car to boost employment.
Hartnett resigned in 1948 shortly before the car, the
Holden 48/215, was unveiled.*

I received your letter of 4th July and your idea of inquiring of what
people read when they were young is excellent. Unfortunately
the books available and popular when I was young some seventy
years or more ago are probably out of date or old-fashioned.

However, to answer your letter, from my memory: *Robinson
Crusoe*, written by Daniel Defoe, which I read many times,
followed by *Swiss Family Robinson*. Then in the age bracket that
you are dealing with Jules Verne *Around the World in 80 Days*
and others; Ryder Haggard *King Solomon's Mines*; Conan Doyle
Sherlock Holmes; *The Speckled Band, Hound of the Baskervilles*
followed by African War books such as *Captain Desmond V.C., A
Dash for Khartoum*.

From 9 to 16 years of age, I was educated at one of the old English Public Schools, Epsom College, of medical foundation with a good library. An excellent custom was that masters voluntarily from time to time as it suited them, acted as librarians and influenced boys to select books. As I had a leaning towards the sciences, I invariably waited for a science master to show me the way and for some reason I had indicated to me books on China. I was about 14 years and the subject fascinated me with the result when asked in the Upper Fourth form to write an essay on one's own choice, I wrote on China and to my surprise received a special prize entitled *Engineering of Today* by Thomas W. Corbin published by Seeley and Company of London. This book changed my whole outlook as to what I wanted to do, namely engineering. Prior to that it was always assumed by my mother and relations that I would follow my father and be a doctor of medicine. Accordingly the reading of one book changed my life.

Contained within the school library were good magazines like *Blackwoods, The Strand* and always *The Illustrated London News*; which all my life I have continued to read including the present time and have found it a fountain of broad knowledge. A famous monthly was *Boys Own* and in particular *Boys Own Annual* which was extremely popular right across the country and in all forms of living.

The magazines I read and later subscribed to - - *The Motor Cycle, Flight,* and *Aeroplane* and still have scrap books with cuttings from these publications. From a scholastic angle I found pleasure when we were led through the essays of Addison and Steele, whereas Shakespeare Dickens and Tennyson were heavy going for me.

In brief I commend to young fellows: mix your reading, a touch of literature, exciting fiction and connecting a serious hobby with publications that go with it.

Hoping this is of help to you.

Sir Paul Hasluck

1905 – 1993

The Honourable Sir Paul Hasluck, KG, GCMG, GCVO, PC, was born in Fremantle, Western Australia, and attended Perth Modern School and the University of Western Australia. After graduation, he joined the university as a faculty member, eventually becoming a reader in history. He joined the Department of External Affairs during World War II, and served as Australia's first Permanent Representative to the United Nations from 1946 to 1947. In 1949, he was elected to federal parliament for the Liberal Party, winning the seat of Curtin. In 1951, he was made Minister for Territories. He later served as Minister for Defence from 1963 to 1964 and Minister for External Affairs from 1964 to1969. He was appointed Governor-General of Australia, and held office from 1969 to 1974. In retirement, he was a prolific author, publishing an autobiography, several volumes of poetry, and multiple works on Australian history.

Your letter of July 4 has been brought under my notice by my private secretary who acknowledged its receipt by letter dated July 11.

I find some difficulty in giving a short answer to your question: "Which book or books were your favourites or influenced you most as a teenager and why." During those years of my life (1918-1924) I was attending Perth Modern School which was singular among schools of that period in having a good library. I also had easy access to the Perth Public Library which in those days had open shelves; I could borrow books from a Sunday School library and from the libraries of the Guildford Mechanics Institute and the Perth Literary Institute and there were lots of books at home. Consequently I was reading eagerly hundreds of books a year on all sorts of subjects and following wherever my curiosity took me. Perhaps the ones that influenced me were the favourite ones I had among the books we studied intensively in the courses in English at school. They were undoubtedly Chaucer, Shakespeare, Milton and Wordsworth. They certainly remained part of my life throughout the whole of my life. Although some of the teachers I had in secondary school were rather dreary I had the good fortune to have three successive teachers of English literature who loved the subject they taught and inspired their students.

Stanley Hawes

1905 - 1991

Stanley Gilbert Hawes, MBE was a British-born documentary film producer and director who spent most of his career in Australia, though he commenced his career in England and Canada. He was born in London, England and died in Sydney. He is best known as the Producer-in-Chief (1946–1969) of the Australian Government's filmmaking body, which was named, in 1945, the Australian National Film Board, and then, in 1956, the Commonwealth Film Unit. In 1973, after he retired, it became Film Australia. His best-known films are "School in the Mailbox", which had been nominated for an Academy Award as Best Short Documentary, "Flight Plan" and "The Queen in Australia".

I was interested in your letter of July 10. Please excuse this tardy reply which I hope is not too late to be of use to you. It is due to my having been away from home for three weeks.

Your project sounds enterprising and I wish it every success. In due course I would like to know how it prospers and how you choose your guinea-pigs.

It's a little difficult for me to be very precise about my teenage habits particularly as many of my books have disappeared over the years but I hope that the following remarks will be the sort of thing you want:

The who authors, out of many, who most influenced me in my teens were H.G. Wells and Bernard Shaw both of whom at that time were still alive and writing.

I became a Shaw addict in my teenage schooldays when he was still an object of some ridicule among my school-fellows. I saw and read most of his plays, and prefaces, in my teens and early twenties. His conception of the 'life force', probably today unfashionable, had a great effect on me.

Having been influenced by Wells as a boy – I think before my teens – I revelled in his incredible science-fiction romances. *The War of the Worlds, The War in the Air, The Sleeper Awakes* and so on. Then I enjoyed his gay and human novels like *Mr Polly* and *Kipps* and later was stimulated by books like *The Research Magnificent* and *The Undying Fire* (which incidentally is dedicated to All Schoolmasters and Schoolmistresses and every Teacher in the World).

Both authors had great style and command of the language, wit, humour and humanity. In addition they believed in the dignity and courage of the human being; from both came the incentive to live, to the best of one's ability, a life of principle rather than of expediency.

An extract from *The Undying Fire* which parallels the *Book of Job* may clarify what I am trying to say. Job Huss, Headmaster of a modern 'public' school, suffers various adversaries culminating in an operation for supposed cancer. Under the anaesthetic he imagines himself to be tormented by Satan.

Satan: 'Who are you? A pedagogue who gives ill-prepared lessons about history in frowsy classrooms, and dreams that he has been training his young gentlemen to play leap-frog amidst the stars.'

Huss: 'I am a man . . . I am every man who has ever looked up towards the light of God. I am every man who has thought or worked or willed for the race. I am all the explorers and leaders and teachers that man has ever had . . .'

Satan: 'You would plumb the deep of
             knowledge; you would scale the heights
             of space . . . There is no limit to either.'

Huss: 'Then I will plumb and scale for ever. I
             will defeat you.'

I hope that all this does not sound too pretentious and that it will
not sound too pompous to say that I also found the tragedies of
Shakespeare, or some of them, a profound influence, with their
concern for the loftiness of the human spirit and its expression in
sublime language.

Bob Hawke

1929 – 2019

Bob Hawke, AC, was born in Border Town, South Australia. He attended the University of Western Australia and went on to study at University College, Oxford as a Rhodes Scholar. In 1956, He joined the Australian Council of Trade Unions as a research officer and was elected as president of the ACTU in 1969, where he achieved a high public profile. In 1973, he was appointed as president of the Labor Party. In 1980, he was elected to the House of Representatives at the 1980 federal election. Three years later, he was elected unopposed as leader of the Australian Labor Party and led Labor to victory at the 1983 election, and was sworn in as prime minister. He led Labor to victory three times, with successful outcomes in 1984, 1987 and 1990 elections.

I think the book which remains most in my mind from late teenage days is *Clarence Darrow For The Defence*, a biography by Irving Stone.

Even in the hands of Stone, who certainly will not go down as one of the greatest writers of all time, the impact of the subject – Darrow – is overwhelming.

Born in 1837 Darrow, from humble origins rose to the greatest heights as an advocate, not merely in the law, but in a whole range of issues concerning the welfare and advancement of his fellow man. He was an intellectual with the common touch. He had absolute integrity and would fight for the truth as he saw it. The jacket of this book speaks with unerring accuracy where it says: "he again and again defied public opinion and braved the scorn of his friends in order to champion an individual or a cause he believed right. Yet never in all his life did Clarence Darrow become the servant of any man or cause; he practised the truth as he saw it and defended the right wherever he found it". His vision in this sense was not limited to his own country – he was a great internationalist.

If there is a capacity within us to become better human beings, reading the life and thoughts of this great man can, I believe, only stimulate that process.

Bishop John Hazlewood

1924 – 1998

The Right Reverend John Hazlewood was born in London and grew up in New Zealand. He was educated at Nelson College. He served in the Royal Air Force in World War II and then studied theology at King's College, Cambridge. He was ordained in 1949 and, following two curacies in England, he came to Australia where he was curate at Randwick and Dubbo. After a brief return to England, he became Vice-Principal at St Francis College, Brisbane and later a lecturer in ecclesiastical history at the University of Queensland. From 1960 to 1968, he was Dean of St Paul's Cathedral, Rockhampton, and Dean of Perth from 1968 to 1975 when he became Bishop of Ballarat, a post he held until 1993.

Thank you for your letter written far too long ago, in connection with books that influenced me in my teenage years. Herewith a list of the books that Seemed to me to be outstanding at that period of my life. They are a mixed bag of fantasy, occult, war (because it was war time in which I spent my teenage) and what one might call detective fiction. My interest in Shakespeare sprang not only from my love of the English language, but of course because they were frequently school plays in which one was involved. The books are as follows:-

The Cloister and the Hearth. Reid.

The Thin Blue Line. (Battle of Britain)*

The Novels of Dennis Wheatley.

The Novels of Agatha Christie.

The Novels of Dorothy Sayers.

Shakespeare, especially *Hamlet, Merchant of Venice, A Mid-Summer Night's Dream, Othello* and *King Lear.*

Hereward the Wake – Kingsley.

And strangely enough one of the most influential books or two books that took me right through the time I was in the Air Force in the 2nd World War, were A.A. Milne's *Pooh* books, *Winnie the Pooh* and *The House at Pooh Corner.*

What this may reveal of my unfolding character I have no idea and whether it will be of any use or interest to your Year 11 class, I very much doubt.

Please forgive my tardiness in replying to your courteous letter.

*[The author of *The Thin Blue Line* was Charles Graves]

Sir Robert Helpmann

1909 – 1986

Sir Robert Helpmann, CBE, was born at Mt Gambier in South Australia and was educated at Prince Alfred College. He acquired his mother's passion for the theatre and began dancing at a very young age. He was taken on as a student dancer by Anna Pavlova and later joined J.C. Williamson Ltd as a dancer in a wide variety of productions. He travelled to England in 1932 and joined what was to become Sadler's Wells Ballet Company. Whilst still a dancer, he directed a wide variety of plays and operas. He returned to Australia in 1955 with the Old Vic Company. When Peggy van Praagh created the Australian Ballet in 1962, she invited Helpmann to create a new work, "The Display" based around the lyrebird. Back in England in 1964 he directed and choreographed "Camelot". Returning to Australia in 1965 he became co-director of the Australian Ballet. He played a significant role in the Adelaide Festival in 1970 and brought an impressive array of artists to Adelaide to participate. Throughout the 1970s and 1980s he ricocheted between the UK and Australia staging opera, ballet and plays. In 1985, he directed a revival of "The Merry Widow" for the San Diego Opera in the USA. He died in Sydney in 1986.

I apologise for the lateness of my reply to your letter of July 10th. My travelling often means that letters sometimes take a while to reach me and, yours, I'm afraid, only reached me in Melbourne last week. I must congratulate the boys of the Year 11 English class on an excellent idea for a project.

As you can imagine my teenage years were totally taken up with my obsession with the theatre. Consequently the books which influenced me most during those years were all to do with this subject. Of the many I read and enjoyed, two stand out above the rest. They are

Theatre Street by Tamara Kasavina and the autobiography of Ellen Terry.

Naturally the plays of Shakespeare, Shaw and Barrie had an immense interest for me.

Let me wish all the boys every success with their project.

Angas Holmes

1934 – 2014

The Reverend Angas Holmes was born in Adelaide and educated at King's College and the University of Adelaide where he graduated with a Bachelor of Arts degree and a Diploma in Education. Combining teaching at King's College and studying, he completed a Bachelor of Divinity from London University as an external student. After four years at King's, he enrolled at the Berkeley Baptist Divinity School where he completed a Master of Religious Education degree. After positions at Kew Baptist Church and Strathcona Baptist Girls' School, he joined the staff of Prince Alfred College in Adelaide in 1964. His first position as a principal came at Oakburn College in Launceston in 1972. He became Headmaster of Caulfield Grammar School in Melbourne in 1977 where he remained until retirement at the end of 1992.

Your request to me regarding the book or books that influenced me most as a teenager has really set me thinking. The more I thought about your question the more I found that most of the books during my teenage years were connected with study programmes that I had at School or University.

At that time I became familiar with the works of Shakespeare, particularly his tragedies, Thomas Hardy and Charles Dickens. Although these books were set as part of course requirements, I found that they fascinated me because of the insight they gave to human nature and how different characters react to different circumstances.

There were two facets of my teenage development that were

mainly influenced outside of school reading: my own personal philosophy of life, and my love for the study of history. Some of the simpler writings of the Greek philosopher Plato, and the more modern English philosopher, Bertrand Russell, influenced my thinking considerably. But, most importantly, I was influenced by *The Bible.* The Authorised Version was always an important book in our home, but during my teenage years there were published the paraphrase of several books in the New Testament by the English clergyman, J.B. Phillips. His *Letters to Young Churches* suddenly made the teachings of Jesus real to me and relevant to the 20th century.

I have always been very interested in history. As a child I was fascinated by the myths and legends of the Greeks and Romans, particularly the stories of Homer's *Iliad* and *Odyssey.* During my teenage years, I began to read some Australian history but became more and more fascinated with European history.

I cannot pinpoint any particular books during this period of reading, but I found for my relaxation I was reading historical novels. One that particularly sticks in my mind, although it is not strictly a historical novel, is Alexandre Dumas' *The Count of Monte Cristo.* This I found a most exciting story with a complex plot set in a fascinating period of French history.

The reading that I did during my teenage years was really something like fumbling at the locks and door-knobs of several doors in a long corridor. Some doors I found easier to open than others, and, as I ventured inside, I discovered new vistas, new characters, new ideas, all of which I am still exploring.

A.D. Hope

1907 - 2000

Alec Derwent Hope, AC, OBE, was born in Cooma, New South Wales. He was educated partly at home and in Tasmania, where his family moved in 1911. Three years later they moved to Sydney. He attended Fort Street High School, the University of Sydney and the University of Oxford. Returning to Australia in 1931 he then trained as a teacher, and spent some time drifting. He was a lecturer at the University of Melbourne from 1945 to 1950, and in 1951 became the first professor of English at the newly founded Canberra University College, later the Australian National University when the two institutions merged. At the ANU he and Tom Inglis Moore created the first full year course in Australian literature at an Australian university. Although he was published as a poet while still young, "The Wandering Islands" published in 1955 was his first collection and all that remained of his early work after most of his manuscripts were destroyed in a fire. He was referred to in an American journal as "the 20th century's greatest 18th-century poet".

My apologies for not answering your letter before this but I have been away in Sydney on various little jobs.

I don't know how you see the question of 'influence' when I was young as intended to 'improve the reading habits of class 11 boys.' As far as I remember I was at that age mainly engaged in trying to become a first-class cricketer. But I did, I recall, write poems. Which I took great pains to conceal from my sporting mates.

What I read at the time were for the most part the books set for my school course: the ones I remember are a selection of Byron and my first introduction to Ovid. Catullus came a little later and was more enchanting. Does your Year 11 read Latin?

'Teenager' of course is a vague term. At the beginning I was influenced by the writers I have mentioned. By the end I had added Milton, Spenser, Blake, Donne, Pope, T.S. Eliot, Yeats, Ezra Pound, Virgil, Marlowe, Chaucer, Ronsard, Whitman, the Mahabharatas and so on: you name it, I read it. I read everything that came my way, and this is probably the real answer to your teenagers: while you have the chance, read the lot that comes your way; at that age you are as plastic as can be; you can absorb anything; none of it may matter but some of it will take root. Don't worry, have a go!

Peter Howson

1919 – 2009

The Honourable Peter Howson, CMG, was born in London and educated at Stowe and Trinity College, Cambridge, graduating with the degree of Master of Arts. He joined the Fleet Air Arm as a pilot and served in the Mediterranean and survived being shot down over Malta. After the war, he came to Australia to join Foy and Gibson, a firm established by his grandfather. He joined the Liberal Party in 1948 and was elected, in 1955, to the Seat of Fawkner and later Casey. He served as Minister for Air and later as Minister for the Environment, Aborigines and the Arts. He lost his seat in 1972 but continued his involvement with the Liberal Party and devoted himself to charitable works, on the Victorian and Australian Deafness Council and became chairman of the Eye and Ear Hospital in the early 1980s. He published his diaries "The Life of Politics" in 1984.

I recall that T.H. White joined the staff at Stowe as English Tutor on the same day that I entered the school, in September 1932. We were in the Scholarship form and he was tutoring us in the set books for the School Certificate, Shakespeare's *Hamlet* and Chaucer's *Prologue for the Canterbury Tales.*

One of his first essays concerned Malory's *Le Morte D'Arthur.* He was always keen on the Arthurian legends and these became the inspiration for some of the books that he was writing at the time. Two of White's books that I remember well were *The Sword in the Stone;* and *England Have My Bones*, which records some of his experiences at Stowe.

He used to enjoy Falconry and he kept a range of animals in his study, including snakes. He drove an old Bentley: I can remember the thrill of being driven in it at one hundred miles an hour for the first time.

I can remember his statement early on that if any of us decided to specialise in English, he could assure us of a scholarship to Cambridge. I always regret that I didn't take him up on it.

Barry Humphries

1934 - 2023

Barry Humphries, AC, CBE, was born in Kew and educated at Melbourne Grammar School and the University of Melbourne. He is sometimes described as "an Australian comedian" but that barely does him justice. His "Who's Who" entry gives his occupation as "Actor; Writer; Music Hall Artiste" and that is getting closer to the mark. He is probably best known for writing and playing two of his creations: Dame Edna Everage (who appeared on five Australian postage stamps in 2006) and Sir Les Patterson – once seen never forgotten. Barry Humphries was the author of more than 15 books, many of which amplify the characters he portrayed on stage. He had won multiple awards and, in 1997, was named as an Australian National Treasure.

My present reading habits were formed while I was a student at Melbourne Grammar in the late '40s and early '50s and the tastes I formed then seem to have persisted. Remember that Melbourne was and still is a city in which anything resembling a literary or artistic atmosphere was conspicuous by its absence. Here are some of the books I liked then:

Main Street by Sinclair Lewis. Although Lewis was a best seller in his time, i.e. the '20s, he has not been the subject of a fashionable revival like F. Scott Fitzgerald. I remember enjoying *Main Street* because it seemed to be about the conflict between artistic inclinations and oppressive small town philistines: a conflict which any sensitive person growing up in Australia must feel acutely.

I also liked the poems of Siegfried Sassoon, particularly his first world war satires. A lot of my early verse was written in imitation of Sassoon and Sitwell and in those days one heard a lot of cant about the virtues of war time sacrifice, particularly from old retired military types on Anzac Day. I also read Sassoon's prose autobiography *Memoirs of an Infantry Officer.*

Three Lives by Gertrude Stein. This is an early book by that extraordinary American writer and it is probably her most readable. If it is not in paperback it should be as it is one of the most important books of the 20th Century and contains three of the most profound and compassionate prose portraits of women I have read. It influenced my early monologues.

Father and Son by Edmund Gosse. This is about the best book anyone has ever written about a parent. It is worth reading for its last sentence.

Melmoth the Wanderer by Maturin (in Penguin). There used to be an old bookseller in Prahran with an amazing stock of early 19th Century fiction, most of it 'gothic'. The best of all this school is Melmoth which has a wonderful surrealistic atmosphere. It is as important as another of my gothic favourites, *Vathek* by William Beckford.

I never read any Australian books at all. They all reminded me of heat, dust, stale sandwiches, and blow-flies, and mostly they still do. Exceptions are *For the Term of his Natural Life* by Marcus Clarke, *The Fortunes of Richard Mahoney* by Henry Handel Richardson. Most Australian novels are a bit like Australian films – a lot of trouble taken and no story worth telling.

Robert Ingpen

Born 1936

Robert Ingpen, AM, FRSA, MSIA, was born in Geelong and attended The Geelong College. He graduated with a Diploma of Graphic Art from RMIT in 1958 when he was appointed by the CSIRO as an artist to interpret and communicate the results of scientific research. From 1968, he worked as a freelance designer, illustrator and author. His interest in conservation issues continued, and he was one of the founding members of the Australian Conservation Foundation.

He has written or illustrated more than 100 published books. These include children's picture books and fictional stories for all ages. His nonfiction books mostly relate to history, conservation, environment and health issues. He has designed many postage stamps for Australia, as well as the flag and coat of arms for the Northern Territory. He also has designed bronze works, which include the bronze doors to the Melbourne Cricket Club. His most recent work is the design and working drawings for a tapestry, which was woven by The Victorian Tapestry Workshop, to celebrate the 150 years of the Melbourne Cricket Ground.

Apart from congratulating your class on devising such an interesting and motivating idea for an English project, I reply by saying that, without any doubt, my favourite book even as a teenager was Norman Lindsay's *The Magic Pudding.*

The range of books in those days stretched from *Biggles* to Thomas Hardy and beyond, yet I remained absorbed by the fantasy and basic honesty of Bunyip Bluegum, Sam Sawnoff and Barnacle Bill – owners of the 'cut-and-come-again' Magic Pudding.

In my recent book, *Australian Gnomes* I paid homage to my teacher (unofficial) Margery Wood. She told wonderful stories none of which was ever written or published, yet the effect of her storytelling has remained very strong with me, although I would hardly have admitted that in my teenage times.

Peter Isaacson

1920 - 2017

Wing Commander Peter Isaacson, AM, DFC, AFC, DFM, was born in London and came to Melbourne at the age of six. He was educated at Brighton Grammar School and the University of Melbourne. He enlisted in the RAAF in 1940 and joined the RAF Pathfinder Squadron in 1943, serving with distinction in many sorties over Europe. After the war, he launched a successful business publishing newspapers, business and professional journals.

My authors when I was a young teenager were Captain W.E. Johns and Percy F. Westerman – the former writer of the Biggles books and the latter a series of books on the merchant marine.

The Billabong series were another of my favourites.

From about 14 onwards I was a keen reader of biographies and autobiographies – none of which stand out specifically as being an influence on my life but all of which I am sure added something to my knowledge of the world and of human behaviour.

It may not surprise you to know I have always read newspapers – and my favourite occupation whether here or abroad is browsing in book shops.

Kenneth Jack

1924 – 2006

Kenneth Jack, AM, MBE, was born in Malvern and educated at Melbourne High School and Royal Melbourne Technical College. During the war, he served in the RAAF in New Guinea and Borneo then became an art teacher in a number of schools. He became a professional painter at the age of 39 after giving up his job as senior instructor at the Caulfield Institute of Technology and continued as a prolific painter until his death. He specialised in painting the images of an almost forgotten outback life: old mine workings, ghost towns, decaying farm buildings.

Thank you for our letter of July 25th telling of the interesting project your Year 11 English class has devised.

Firstly you have chosen someone who doesn't read a great deal – I am a professional artist (landscape) and since my childhood have been more interested in the visual aspects of this world. The art and architecture of man and the beauties of nature expressed in art and felt by me in nature itself have always taken more of my time than reading. When others would be reading I would prefer to be drawing or painting. And, to be frank, after painting and drawing, fine music has always interested me more than fine literature.

So therefore you have in me someone talking to you who is really no great expert at all and my reply will certainly be different to all other you receive.

I am in my mid-fifties so my teenage was from about 1937 to

1945 (3 years were spent in awkward situations at the war in New Guinea and beyond – aged 18, 19 and 20, where nothing much in the way of books was available).

These are books I definitely remember as being important:

The Bible

A Tale of Two Cities and other works of Dickens

Works of Dumas (I still enjoy an adventure story)

History of Architecture by Sir Banister Fletcher (a huge volume profusely illustrated with hundreds of photos & drawings, plans, cross-sections, elevations, etc. of world architecture and to which I still refer frequently – the first copy I used was owned by my father who was an also an artist)

Advertising and British Art – another profusely illustrated book also owned by my father.

Modern World Encyclopaedia (9 volumes owned by parents)

The Treasury of Knowledge (published in England about 1933 and given to me in 1934 and which I still have)

The Physiography of Victoria by E. Sherbon Hills (profusely illustrated with photos and diagrams of how our landscape was geologically formed)

National Geographic Magazines

Walkabout (Australia's geographic magazine)

John Keats – I remember the wonderful poetic visual imagery in his poems – they impressed me above all others in the field.

Hope this will be of some small use to your class. Good luck with your project and your studies.

Sir Robert Jackson

1911 – 1991

Sir Robert Jackson, AC, KCVO, CMG, OBE, was born in Melbourne and was educated at Cheltenham High School and Mentone Grammar School. He joined the Royal Australian Navy at 18. He was seconded to the Royal Navy in 1938 and proved his ability in his plans for defending Malta during the Second World War. After the war, Jackson was responsible for the United Nations Relief and Rehabilitation Administration projects in Europe, parts of Africa and the Far East before moving to the Australian Ministry of National Development. From the 1950s onward, he advised the governments of India and Pakistan, and in 1962 he went to the UN as consultant to the United Nations Development Programme, advising on technical, logistical and pre-investment aid to developing countries. His last major operations were co-ordinating relief for Bangladesh between 1972 and 1975, and assistance for Kampuchea and Kampuchean refugees in Thailand between 1979 and 1984.

Your letter of 25 July reached me, by chance, in Moscow and I am dictating this quick answer before returning to Indo-China. I have given considerable thought to your question whilst flying during the last few days, and I have come to the conclusion that my favourite books, as a teenager, also had a direct influence on the rest of my life.

I think I have always been curious about the world in which we live and, therefore, during that period of my life – now over 50 years ago – I was always on the lookout for books of general knowledge. Against that broad background, I was particularly interested – as I am to this day – in action, either in romantic fiction (obviously *Robinson Crusoe* and Treasure *Island* come into that category) or action in fact, as reflected in records of explorations (Captain James Cook, Captain Robert Scott and Antarctica, Amundsen, etc.) in this century, while others such as Nelson and Napoleon at an earlier stage, and the great heroes of the past, all had a special place in my reading. So too, did autobiographies and biographies; as I grew older, I became more interested in political action and the role of statesmen (in contrast to politicians) in influencing the conduct of affairs and history.

Of course, having said that, there has always been the certain basic reading. For most people, I assume that *The Bible* still plays a special role (whether they believe or not) and the same would hold good of Shakespeare, particularly in terms of human behaviour expressed both in terms of its strengths and frailties.

I do not know whether these comments may be of any interest to your boys, but early reading certainly had a direct influence on the rest of my life which, most people seem to think, has been exceedingly varied and rich in experience.

Sir Asher Joel

1912 – 1998

Sir Asher Joel, KBE, AO, was born in Sydney and educated at Enmore Public School and Cleveland Street High School. He started work as a copyboy at Sydney's Daily Telegraph. In 1937, he joined the New South Wales committee organising the Australian celebration of the coronation of King George VI. He joined the army in 1942 but, later in the same year, transferred to the Navy and served on General Douglas MacArthur's war agency staff. In 1946, he was instrumental in the establishment of the Public Relations Institute of Australia.

He masterminded many huge events, including visits to Sydney by The Queen and Duke of Edinburgh in 1963, President Lyndon Johnson in 1966 and Pope Paul in 1970. He oversaw the Captain Cook bicentenary events in 1970 and the opening of the Sydney Opera House. He was elected to the NSW Legislative Council as an independent in 1958, but joined the Country Party the following year. He was a founder and governor of the Australia-Israel Chamber of Commerce. After retiring from politics in 1978, he wrote the book "Australian Protocol and Procedures".

What an interesting project has been devised by your pupils. I am sure that some of the comments will be really worthwhile.

It is so long since I was a teenager that I am rather reluctant to express views such as those you hope to seek. But perhaps the following will suffice. I hope so.

Two authors of plays rather than books made a strong impression upon me in the years approaching manhood. They are Henrik Ibsen and George Bernard Shaw. Both had an infinite capacity to direct attention to social conditions and the play and emotional stresses of human behaviour.

Ibsen's *Ghosts* and *The Dolls House* gave penetrating insights into human behaviour. Shaw fearlessly in his works, such as *The Doctor's Dilemma*, tears away the facades of pseudo-respectability, exposing sham and hypocrisy.

Dostoyevsky's *Crime and Punishment*, a magnificent psychological drama, disturbing because of its grim reality and the superb portrayal of the characters, also made a profound impression on me.

It is important in reading such works, however, not to become too cynical; they should be regarded as the foundation for a better personal understanding of human behaviour, and the weaknesses and strengths of our fellow man.

I trust the project is successful in achieving such a stimulating aim, and I thank you and the boys of your class for paying me the compliment of seeking my views.

Ian Johnson

1917 – 1998

Ian Johnson, CBE, was born in North Melbourne and educated at Wesley College. He found his vocation in cricket. In 1934–35, aged only 16, and still a schoolboy, he played his first match for the South Melbourne Cricket Club First XI and made his debut for Victoria in the 1935-36 season. His career was interrupted by the Second World War; he served with the RAAF as a pilot and later as a flight instructor. He returned to cricket after his discharge and was selected to tour New Zealand with the Australian team, making his Test debut. Johnson was part of Don Bradman's Invincibles team; undefeated on tour in England in 1948. he retired from all forms of cricket at age 39.

After retirement, Johnson worked for a time as a sports commentator, including covering the 1956 Summer Olympics in Melbourne. In 1957 he was appointed Secretary of the Melbourne Cricket Club, one of the most prestigious positions in Australian sport. He would remain in the role for 26 years, overseeing the development of the MCG and playing a key role in the organisation of the Centenary Test in 1977.

I acknowledge receipt of your letter of July 25th and must admit to a little difficulty in remembering the books I read in my teenage days. They are a long time past!

As I recall it my two favourite authors for leisure reading at that time were Rafael Sabatini and P.C. Wren. The first because the stories were romantic period adventures with a colourful smattering of loose history. Sabatini had an elegant style of writing which also impressed me and his plots, although on reflection a little simple, were most intriguing in my teen years.

P.C. Wren I liked because of the strong and positive expression of the writing and also because a sense of loyalty and morality were the main themes of his writings. I recall one other character – and I forget which – saying that his motto was "I say – I do". Another said that "Courage is not being without fear, it is being able to overcome the fear you have. Where there is no fear there is no courage nor any need of it". I must say that both those quotes made a lasting impression on me.

Of course I also loved Shakespeare. I was fortunate in having an outstanding English master – Jock Hargreaves – who really taught me an appreciation of the bard. Following his advice, I never read the works silently but always went to my room, sat down, and read aloud to myself. I still believe that this is the only way to obtain full enjoyment of the power and beauty of expression of this master artist. As has so often been said as to become a cliché – "It is amazing the number of well known quotations Shakespeare used in his writings!".

This strength and beauty by just one example. The common misquotation – "A rose by any other name would smell as sweet." Compare this with Shakespeare's original "That which we call a rose by any other name would smell as sweet." The meaning is just the same but the beauty . . . . . . !

One could call on many other of his famous lines. Modern English can rarely be described, as Keats once said (of the Nightingale was it – or the Grecian Urn? "A thing of beauty is a joy forever". Shakespeare certainly made the English language just that.

Barry Jones

Born 1932

Professor the Honourable Barry Jones, AC, FAA, first came to fame as a quiz champion. He was educated at Melbourne High School and the University of Melbourne where he graduated in Arts and Law. At various times he has been a teacher, public servant, lecturer, lawyer and entered the Victorian Parliament in 1972. In 1977, he transferred to the Australian Parliament as Member for Lalor, holding the seat until 1998. He was Minister for Science from 1983 to 1990, Prices and Consumer Affairs in 1987, Small Business from 1987 to 1990 and Customs from 1988 to 1990. He served on the Executive Board of UNESCO in Paris from 1991 to 1995 and was Vice-President of the World Heritage Committee from 1995 to 1996. He was twice National President of the Australian Labor Party, from 1992 to 2000 and from 2005 to 2006. He is the author of a number of significant works including "Sleepers Wake! Technology and the Future of Work" published in 1982, "Barry Jones' Dictionary of World Biography" first published in 1994 and his autobiography "A Thinking Reed" in 2006.

When I was a sub-teenager, and probably into my early teens as well, my favourite author was Hendrik van Loon (1882 – 1944), a Dutch writer living in the U.S. His books, *The Story of Mankind, The Home of Mankind* and *The Liberators of Mankind* shaped my general approach to human society very deeply. I was also very much addicted to G.B. Shaw, H.G. Wells and Jules Verne (especially *Around the World in 80 Days* which I must have read at least ten times).

Marilyn Jones

Born 1940

Marilyn Jones, OBE, was born in England and educated at the Newcastle Home Science High School. She studied ballet with Tessa Maunder in Newcastle then at the Royal Ballet School in London and danced with the Royal Ballet from 1957 to 1958. She was a principal artist with the Borovansky Ballet and was invited to join its successor, the Australian Ballet as a founding principal in 1962. She danced with the Australian Ballet as a prima ballerina until 1978, when she took up the position of Artistic Director of the company from 1979 to 1982. After receiving a Creative Arts Fellowship from the Australian Government, Jones founded the Australian Institute of Classical Dance in 1991 and became its artistic director. The AICD was set up to oversee and encourage the development of classical dance in Australia. Other appointments have included director of the National Theatre Youth Ballet from 1996 to 1998, and Director of the National Theatre Ballet School in Melbourne from 1995 to 1998. She taught at the Western Academy of Performing Arts from 1999 to 2001. She has been described as "the greatest classical dancer Australia has produced".

Thank you for your letter of July 25. I am sorry that my touring commitments with the company have precluded my earlier reply.

I found, as a teenager, that I was influenced by the works of Charles Dickens, Thomas Hardy, Jane Austen and the Bronte sisters. Their works gave powerful descriptions of society, its problems and its manners.

I felt that knowledge so acquired helped me considerably to appreciate contemporary society and the problems which confront it. It does help to get an overall picture of mankind.

Louis Kahan

1905 – 2002

Louis Kahan, AO, was born in Vienna and initially trained as a tailor with his father. He was particularly drawn to art and sketched his father's clients. In 1925 he travelled from Vienna to Paris where he worked with couturier Paul Poiret, first as a tailor and then designer. He enlisted in the French Foreign Legion in 1939 and was sent to Algeria as a war artist. He had an exhibition at Oran in 1942. He returned to Paris after the war and was employed by Le Figaro to sketch the court scenes of the war trials. After travelling across the United States he moved to Perth to join his family, who had emigrated to Australia before the war. In Perth he had his first solo exhibition and began to be recognized by the art world, with work purchased by the Art Gallery of Western Australia. He moved to Melbourne in 1950 where his talent for portraiture was recognized by Melbourne Herald art critic Alan McCulloch, who introduced him to the editor of "Meanjin". He made many portraits of Australian and other celebrities. He collaborated with producer Stephen Haag, designing sets and costumes for opera and theatre. The Victorian Art Centre, Melbourne, has a large collection of his portraits of musicians, and set and costume designs. He won the Archibald Prize in 1962 with a portrait of Patrick White.

I apologize for the delay in answering our letter of 25/7 which is due to my absence from Melbourne & my subsequent short illness. I hope it doesn't come too late for your purpose. Although I have always been active in sports (Hockey & Skiing) I was also a great bookworm at a very early age.

Like most boys – I presume – I liked books about adventure &
travels which stimulated my imagination:

Friedrich Gerstäcker, *Gulliver's Travels*, books which appealed to
my sense of humour like Jerome K. Jerome's *Three Men in a Boat*,
Twain's *Yankee at King Arthur's Court*, *The Pickwick Papers,* or
Munchausen's Travels (which one could call absurd surrealism).
But I also was fascinated by A.E. Poe's which are every bit as.

But above all I was looking for books on art, on which my
grounding as an artist is based. I didn't go to Art School.

Peter Karmel

1922 - 2008

Professor Peter Karmel, AC, CBE, was educated at Caulfield Grammar School, the University of Melbourne and Cambridge University. After working at the Commonwealth Bureau of Census and Statistics in Canberra, he accepted a lectureship in Economics and Economic History at the University of Melbourne in 1946. At the age of 27, he was appointed to the chair of economics at the University of Adelaide in 1950. His economic research included a focus on educational issues. In 1971 he moved back to Canberra to head the Australian Universities Commission, becoming chairman and head of its successor, the Commonwealth Tertiary Education Commission. Professor Karmel released a 1973 report commissioned by the Whitlam government named "Schools in Australia" which influenced the government)s funding of state schools. He was Vice-Chancellor of the Australian National University from 1982 to 1987.

Thank you for your letter of 25th July.

I have delayed answering because I do not find a response all that easy; my memory is not the strongest at the best of times, and to recall reading habits or rather more than 40 years ago puts it to a great test.

However, I can say quite briefly that, while I have always read a great deal, I do not recall any particular book as having a special influence on me. While in senior school and at university, studying occupied much of my time; apart from this, I read as much as I could of English, French and Russian novelists of the 18th and 19th centuries: Sterne (*Tristram Shandy*), Fielding (*Tom Jones*), Thackeray (*Vanity Fair*), Dickens (*Our Mutual Friend*), Balzac (*Droll Stories*), Hugo (*Les Miserables*), Tolstoy (*Anna Karenina*), and Dostoieffsky (*Crime and Punishment*).

You will see that I have taken the precaution of not including modern novelists because of the risk of perpetrating an anachronism!

I hope this is of some help.

Nancy Keesing

1923 – 1993

Nancy Keesing, AM, was born in Sydney and attended school at Sydney Girls' Grammar School and Frensham School. During World War 2, she worked as a naval account clerk on Garden Island in Sydney Harbour. After the war, she enrolled in social sciences at the University of Sydney and then worked as a social worker at the Royal Alexandra Hospital for Children at Camperdown from 1947 to1951. From 1952, she worked full-time as a writer and researcher with The Bulletin magazine. She mainly worked with Douglas Stewart, particularly to research and collect historical Australian songs and bush ballads. Her literary career covered several fields, including poetry, literary criticism, editing, children's novels and biography. One of her most well-known works is "Shalom", a collection of Australian Jewish stories. She wrote or edited 26 volumes and wrote two memoirs: "Garden Island People", about her work on Garden Island, and "Riding the Elephant", mainly about her literary career.

Your letter of 25th July has arrived just as I'm clearing my desk to be away for a couple of weeks. If I don't answer it quickly goodness knows when I'll get to it, so forgive a somewhat top-of-the-muddled-head response.

Childhood books would have been easier to list than teenage ones. By the time I was nineteen I was spending nearly two hours in a train travelling to work each day and reading a lot of books as I've done, anyway, since I learned to read at four.

Well, to take the plunge. From about 11 – 15 anything in the parental bookshelves from left to right across five rows including all Kipling, some Jane Austen, all William J. Locke, all Thomas Burke, some early Priestly, some early Norman Douglas.

My father brought home a strap-full of books from a lending library each week and his tastes were historical fiction and also for American fiction - - so Hemingway, Steinbeck, Falkiner, Willa Cather, Eudora Welty, *Gone with the Wind*.

Poetry: Leon Gellert's *Songs of a Campaign* which I discovered when I was about 8 and read often ever since; *The Oxford Book of Modern Verse* (ed. W.B. Yeats) which I was given when I was 14 or 15 and which seduced me to 20th century poetry thereafter. I bought many of the poets therein when I could afford to.

Eliot, Auden and Spender and Day Lewis etc. were beginning to be widely read in my school days and our rather "advanced" English teacher introduced them - - again I bought their books.

The Tempest, The Merchant of Venice (both studied intensively and enjoyed and remembered.) I did have very good teachers and was never "turned off" books we studied in class.

Anything banned was a firm favourite so - - *Brave New World, Ulysses,* an opus called *Twinkletoes* by Thomas Burke, Norman Lindsay's *Redheap* and *Saturdee,* and a novel about American brothels called *The Daughters of Ishmael.*

Katherine Mansfield. The Brontes. And Donn Byrne whom all my generation swooned over, virtually. Can still enjoy *Destiny Bay.*

Lytton Strachey and other biographers. Little Australian (though much Australian work in pre-teenage reading). I don't think my father thought much of Aust. books and what he brought home or what the school library offered was what one chiefly read. Then when I was 18 I attended some WEA classes in Aust. Lit. (tutored by H.M. Green) and after that every Aust. Writer of the period

I could get my hands on - - Tennant, Dark, Prichard, etc. etc. & Slessor, FitzGerald, Douglas Stewart etc. Rosemary Dobson was a school friend.

Have omitted Dorothy Sayers et al. The hey-day of detective stories & we read them avidly.

Good wishes to your class and you.

Michael Kirby

Born 1939

The Honourable Michael Kirby, AC, CMG, was born in Sydney and educated at North Strathfield Public School, Summer Hill Public School, Fort Street High School and the University of Sydney, graduating with the degrees of Bachelor of Arts, Bachelor of Economics and Master of Laws. He worked as a solicitor until joining the New South Wales Bar in 1967. In 1975, he became the youngest person appointed to federal judicial office when he became Deputy President of the Australian Conciliation and Arbitration Commission and Chairman of the Australian Law Reform Commission. He was appointed a judge of the Federal Court in 1983 and, in 1984, became President of the New South Wales Court of Appeal. In 1996 he was appointed a Justice of the High Court of Australia, retiring in 2009. The United Nations Human Rights Council appointed him in 2013 to lead a commission of inquiry into human rights abuses in North Korea for which the Japanese government awarded him the Order of the Rising Sun. He is an honorary professor of 12 universities, holds 29 honorary degrees and is an Australian Living National Treasure. He is a vocal advocate for gay rights.

When I was at school, the book that chiefly influenced me, in a broad way, was the set of encyclopaedias published by Arthur Mee. I had seen them in the home of a neighbour and was ultimately able to persuade my parents, who were rather poor, to purchase them for me. I suppose that my strong Anglophile tendencies were in part a product of reading history, geography, the sciences and above all literature through the eyes of English authors. In retrospect, I imagine these volumes nowadays would look like an Imperial relic. They had been written in the 1930s and in the post-War economies were largely reproduced unaltered with the merest post-script for the Second World War. Accordingly, in the 1950s I was reading the safe world of the Empire before vastly changing moral and social values, the growth of government, the growth of big business and the impact of science and technology.

In 1955 I sat for the Leaving Certificate at Fort Street High School in Sydney. This is a famous school which has produced many great Australians, including such figures as Barton, Barwick, Kerr, Spender, Dr Evatt, Ellicott, Wran and so on.

The Shakespeare set for the Leaving Certificate in 1955 was *Julius Caesar*. My father purchased a record of the film which had then been recently released in which John Gielgud, Marlon Brando, James Mason and others took part. This record, which I played repeatedly, drummed into my mind the magnificent beauty of oral Shakespeare. Shakespeare is not a thing to be read in books alone. I recommend to students that they should learn Shakespeare from records and cassettes spoken by great actors and actresses. I went on to buy other records and still find great enjoyment from listening to them and from being able to quote large sections of Shakespeare as a living dramatic force.

In fact, I was the first generation of the electronic age. In future, books will become less important in life and in teaching. We will all adapt to the electronic instruments of communication. I strongly recommend taking this leap, especially where our poetry and literature are concerned. The strength of the civilisation of The Netherlands is painting. The great strength of German civilisation is music. The strength of the English-speaking people is literature, government and laws.

Sir Richard Kirby

1904 - 2001

Sir Richard Kirby, AC, was born in Sydney and educated at The King's School and the University of Sydney where he graduated in law. He was a District Court judge from 1944 to 1947 and an acting judge of the Supreme Court in 1947. He was a member of the Australian War Crimes Commission and from 1956 to 1973 he was president of the Australian Commonwealth Conciliation and Arbitration Commission. He became chairman of the Advertising Standards Council in 1973.

I was flattered by your letter of 7 August regarding the books I liked most in my teens and why. I have to search my mind to recollect, not so much the books I read in those long off days, but why.

The books I liked most, and read over and over again, were three novels by Winston Churchill, not the statesman but an American novelist of the same names. The books were *The Crisis* and *The Crossing* both about U.S. history and *The Celebrity,* a humorous character sketch which amused and puzzled me as I recollect. Strangely enough I haven't read the books since I left school but I still remember the pleasure they gave me when young. I will probably now try to get copies to read again.

I think my reading of those books was inspired by having read and enjoyed North American books by Nancy Johnston and a tear jerker called *The Perfect Tribute* by Mary Raymond Shipman Andrews which recounted a (probably fictional) story about Abraham Lincoln and his granting a pardon to a civil war youthful soldier allegedly guilty of cowardice. Lincoln sat by the dying soldier's bedside, as I recollect and read the Gettysburg address which had a profound effect on the youthful Kirby and still has on the septuagenarian writing this letter.

Good fortune to your good self, your year 11 English boys and their project.

Dame Leonie Kramer

1924 – 2016

Dame Leonie Kramer, AC, DBE, was born in Melbourne and educated at Presbyterian Ladies' College, the University of Melbourne and Oxford University. She was appointed a lecturer in English in 1958, then senior lecturer and finally an associate professor in English at the University of New South Wales. She remained there until 1968, when she was appointed Professor of Australian Literature at the University of Sydney, the first female professor of English in Australia. She was Visiting Professor at Harvard University's Chair of Australian Literature Studies in 1981and 1982. A major focus of her critical writing was the works of Henry Handel Richardson. She also edited the "Oxford History of Australian Literature". She was the first woman to be appointed to the Chair of the Australian Broadcasting Corporation from 1982 to 1983.

I am very sorry not to have replied to your request earlier. Since your letter reached me, I have been out of Sydney almost continuously. I fear that the project will already have been completed, but for what it is worth here is my response.

Your question made me think very hard, and it also made me realize how much reading habits have changed over the years. First, I am sure that I was influenced by poetry than by fiction, and so it is difficult for me to nominate one book which was a particular favourite, or which had a particular influence. But if I were to do so the book would probably be Palgrave's *Golden Treasury of English Poetry* which I read and re-read, and from which I learned to appreciate a wide range of styles and forms in poetry. I suppose it made me think of poetry, as I have continued to think of it, as first of all giving great pleasure through its sound and imagery and tone.

There were particular poets whose work I studied as a teenager – and those I chiefly remember are Milton, Shelley, Shakespeare, and since I was studying Latin, Virgil, Ovid and Horace. In fact I think it was because we read a good deal of Latin poetry, that my very early taste for English poetry was strengthened.

Your question also makes me realize that very few novels that I read in my teenage years made anything like the same impression on me. So perhaps I should rest my answer in poetry.

Once again, please accept my apologies for replying so late. If the project is completed, perhaps my comments still have some interest for your students.

Stanley Kurrle

1922 – 2016

The Reverend Canon Stanley Kurrle, OBE, was born in Victoria, the son of a German immigrant winemaking family. He attended Caulfield Grammar School before going to Melbourne University to read medicine. In October 1940, he enlisted with the 5th Battalion Victorian Scottish Regiment, and spent much of his war service in Western Australia. An army chaplain suggested he consider studying for the ministry. He was discharged in 1944 and returned to Melbourne University to complete a Bachelor of Arts and a Diploma in Education. He then moved to England where he read theology at Oxford, graduating with the degree of Master of Arts. In 1955, he was appointed headmaster of Caulfield Grammar School in Melbourne. Then, in 1965, he became Headmaster of The King's School, Parramatta, founded in 1831. He hit the ground running, with his usual drive and enthusiasm. Retiring in 1983, he devoted himself to running his wife's pastoral property at Mathoura in the Riverina.

I have done my best to try and recall the books which I enjoyed as a teenager. My memory has failed me completely. I am able to remember the titles of books read in primary school but, strangely, cannot recall books read during the next five or six years.

My parents encouraged me to read *The Bulletin* and the daily papers which were, I think, *The Argus* and *The Herald*. I also remember reading *Smiths Weekly* on occasions.

I belonged to two libraries, one conducted by Myers, the other in Glenhuntly Road, Elsternwick and borrowed from both on a regular basis. I also borrowed books from the school library. However, I regret that I cannot recall the name of one title!

John La Nauze

1911 - 1990

John La Nauze was born in the Goldfields town of Boulder, Western Australia. He was educated at South Perth Primary School, Perth Modern School, the University of Western Australia and, as Rhodes Scholar for 1931, at Balliol College, Oxford before joining the Economics Departments at Adelaide University from 1935 and Sydney University from 1940 to 1949. In 1950, he became Foundation Professor of Economic History in the University of Melbourne, moving to the newly created Ernest Scott Chair in the Department of History in 1956. In 1966 he succeeded Sir Keith Hancock as Professor of History in the Institute of Advanced Studies at the Australian National University. On his retirement in 1977 he became the first Professor of Australian Studies at Harvard University in 1978. In the Melbourne History Department, he introduced courses in Later British History – which he believed essential to an understanding of Australian History — and fostered research in both fields.

Reading – I assume that 'teenager' means, or meant in my case, ages 13 - 17½ i.e. before University matriculation, but I was a besotted reader by the time I was seven or eight. As I gobbled up everything which came my way in those years it is difficult to name 'a' favourite book, or even now, to remember precisely what type of authors succeeded one another. Broadly, it seems clear to me that by 13 my tastes in reading had settled down in three ways (1) imaginative fiction (2) English lyric poetry seemed in some way 'better' (more satisfactory to me) than the Australian – ballad verse which had once attracted us at primary school (3) I found a fascination in 'general information' – biography , history, science etc. of the 'encyclopaedic' type – not systematic, but bits of everything. At 13 school added an entirely new 'category' – Shakespearian plays – and I was hooked before I knew that I ought to regard them in this or that way, according to the critic I happen to be reading, at any time during the last fifty years.

I suppose my favourite writers (or at least most read writers) in my 'teens, in these categories, were in the field of 'adventure', action and incident, Kipling, R.L. Stevenson, the Conan Doyle of *Sherlock Holmes* and *Brigadier Gerard*, H.G. Wells of the science fiction period.

In poetry Keats, Coleridge, Tennyson, Swinburne, and a mass of lyrics from Palgrave's *Golden Treasury* & *The Oxford Book of English Verse* – adequately romantic – 'modern' poetry came later, at the University (though not of course in the syllabus).

In prose, Macaulay's Essays and (curious combination) Lamb's Essays – I think led on to extracts from some book of snippets.

For fun, Poe's Tales, Chesterton's *The Club of Queer Trades*, O'Henry, Jack London, etc. etc., anything found in the bookshelves of parents or friends. A marvellous loan from a schoolmaster who was not the teacher of the subject – A.C. Bradley's *Shakespearian Tragedy.*

Why? 'Influence' in a practical sense was mainly in making me at an early age an unusually 'rapid' reader. If you gobble books you gradually find that ways of writing ('style') differs somehow, and some books can be red again & again all your life. And new writing fits somehow into a long and indefinitely extended field of literature.

Australian books? These came later. There would be many now.

Don Lane

1933 – 2009

Broadcaster, show host and comedian Don Lane was born in New York City and educated at DeWitt Clinton High School and Kalamazoo College in Michigan. He was drafted into the army at 21 and became an artillery officer. Recognised as a comedian, he toured army bases entertaining troops after he completed his military service. In 1965, he came to Australia and worked for Channel 9 hosting "Tonight with Don Lane". He returned to the USA in 1969 but came back to Australia to host "The Don Lane Show" from 1975 to 1983, frequently appearing opposite Bert Newton.

From his secretary:

As you may already be aware, Don was brought up in the Bronx, New York. During his teenage years he enjoyed such books as J.D. Salinger's *Catcher in the Rye* and *Call of the Wild* by Zane Grey.

It seems that he enjoyed adventure books, particularly those set in the Wild West; tastes none too extraordinary for a young American boy!

Clifford Last

1918 – 1991

Clifford Last, OBE, was born in Barrow in Furness in England and educated at Barrow Grammar School and the City Guilds Art School in London. He served in the army in World War 2 and was Mentioned in Dispatches. After the war, he emigrated to Melbourne, continued his studies at RMIT and soon became a noted sculptor. He was a foundation member of Centre Five, a group formed in 1960 to promote contemporary abstract sculpture in Australia. Last later was a member of the Commonwealth Art Advisory Board. His work is in gallery collections in Canberra, Melbourne, Ballarat, Mildura and Castlemaine.

The project put up by your Year 11 English class seems highly commendable – trouble is I find it hard to remember clearly what I read in my teens.

Early teenage I lost myself completely in Kipling when my school friends were immersed in the comics of the day. Rider Haggard was my next memory, and I think I worked through all of his many books.

From fifteen to eighteen my interest changed, and I was drawn to historical novels, first Sabatini then Walpole. I still remember his *Rogue Herries* series, perhaps because a lot of action took place in the English Lake District where I spent most of my leisure hours as a boy. Illustrated art books were always included in my withdrawals from the local library though my attempts to copy the work of the artists failed dismally, and turned me away from two-dimensional expression. It wasn't until many years later that

I was fortunate enough to realize that the three-dimensional art of sculpture was how I could express myself.

This is dealt with more fully in the book *Clifford Last* by Max Dimmack. If your school library does not have a copy I would donate one if someone will pick it up.

Wishing the Year 11 English Class success in their project.

Sir Condor Laucke

1914 – 1993

Sir Condor Laucke, KCMG, was born in Greenock, South Australia, and educated at Immanuel College and the School of Mines in Adelaide and, after graduating, joined the family business, becoming Director and General Manager of what was a large milling and stock feed enterprise in 1947. He was elected to the South Australian House of Assembly in the 1956 election, representing the Electoral district of Barossa as part of Sir Thomas Playford's Liberal and Country League government. He was re-elected in 1959 and 1962, and from 1962 to 1965 served as Government Whip. After losing his seat in 1965, he moved into Federal politics, being appointed as a Senator for South Australia to fill the vacancy left by the death of Senator Clive Hannaford, his term beginning on 2 November 1967. He represented South Australia until 1981, being re-elected in 1967, 1974 and 1975, and was President of the Senate from 1976 until 1981. In 1982, he became Lieutenant Governor of South Australia, holding that office until 1992. In 1974, He was one of the founding members of the Barons of Barossa, an organisation formed to promote the Barossa Valley and its winemaking and grape growing industries, to preserve its heritage, traditions and standards, and to carry out philanthropic works.

I thank you for your quite intriguing letter of the 7th inst.

As a primary school boy I found fascination in books written by Edwin S. Ellis as studies in natural environment. Thereafter my greatest pleasures came from reading Charles Dickens which gave me insight into the real problems and difficulties which subsequently led to major social action for betterment in conditions of the people – both parents and children.

Warner's books on Modern History with the assistance of a Master at college who could make history live and major names in political history, human beings of great understanding.

The depiction in Breasted of Ancient History and origins of peoples and nations seemed to give me a rounding of what history is really about.

I found the works of William Shakespeare appealing, particularly when it came to learning of the deep thinking of Shakespeare's characters, e.g. Polonius's advice to his son Laertes in *Hamlet*.

I have found all these writings a jolly fine base for judgement.

You mentioned that a long essay was not required, and I have dictated these few lines spontaneously and hurriedly. I trust they may be of interest to you boys.

Phillip Law

1912 – 2010

Philip Law, AC, CBE, was born in Tallangatta, Victoria. After attending Hamilton High School, he taught in secondary schools, including Melbourne High School where he taught physics and boxing, while studying part-time at the University of Melbourne, earning an MSc in 1941. During the Second World War he enlisted in the RAAF, though the university physics department, which was involved in weapons research, insisted that he continue his work there. He did however manage to visit the battle areas of New Guinea on a four-month scientific mission for the Australian Army. He spent the first of many summers in Antarctica in 1947–8 as a senior research officer on ANARE of which he soon became director. During his directorship, he established bases in Mawson, Davis and Casey, and led expeditions that explored more than 5,000 kilometres of coastline and some 1,000,000 square kilometres of territory. After retiring from the directorship, he chaired the Australian National Committee on Antarctic Research from 1966 to 1980. He was elected President of the Royal Society of Victoria from 1967 to 1968.

You have presented me with a difficult task, trying to remember after a space of 50 years! Let me say that I was an avid reader, always with a book under my pillow so that I could read after I was supposed to be asleep and continue by waking early. I lived in the country and reading (and homework) were the main activities in the evenings. (No radio, no TV.)

At Form 2 level at High School the following represent a fair sample:-

A number of popular English classics published as "Supplementary Readers" by the Education Dept and including adventure stories by R.L. Stevenson, Ballantyne, etc. *Scarlet Pimpernel* series by Baroness Orczy.

Humour by Wodehouse and Jerome K. Jerome (*Three Men in a Boat*) which I thought screamingly funny.

Detective fiction by Edgar Wallace, who also wrote intriguing stories of Africa (*Sanders of the River* series).

Humorous adventure by Dornford Yates *Berry & Co.*

O'Henry's short stories.

By Form 4 and 5 I was reading very adult serious novels.

Never again after the age of 16-17 did I have the opportunity to read as much fiction per year as I did between the ages of 8 and 15. Hopefully I will get back to it again now that I have retired.

I didn't think the sort of reading as a teenager "influenced" me, apart from deepening my love of reading and leading me steadily forward in my appreciation of good literature. Oh yes, I think reading did more to develop my style as a writer and my knowledge of spelling, grammar and syntax than my formal teaching at school!

I hope this will be of some use to you.

Ray Lawler

Born 1921

Ray Lawler, AO, OBE, was born in Footscray. He left school at 13 to work in a foundry and attended evening acting classes. He wrote his first play at 19. In 1955, "Summer of the Seventeenth Doll" was presented by the Union Theatre. The play was taken up by the Australian Elizabethan Theatre Trust and presented in all Australian states as well as London and New York. It was followed by "The Piccadilly Bushman", "The Unshaven Cheek", and "A Breach in the Wall", about St Thomas Becket, which was produced at Canterbury in 1970. Having lived overseas for some years, he visited Australia for the Melbourne Theatre Company's production of his play "The Man Who Shot the Albatross", an impressionistic version of the Governor Bligh story. In 1975, Lawler returned to settle in Australia as associate director of the Melbourne Theatre Company, with an agreement to complete a trilogy based on "Summer of the Seventeenth Doll". The first play, "Kid Stakes", opened in December 1975 and the second, "Other Times", in December 1976. "The Doll Trilogy" had its first full performance at the Russell Street Theatre, Melbourne, on 12 February 1977.

Thank you for your letter of June 5th, inquiring as to my teenage reading.

Looking back, I must confess that I had few particular favourites. I read everything that came to hand. Perhaps it was a period when stories with a strong narrative line and vivid characters had special appeal. I know it was a time when I made full acquaintance with the works of Charles Dickens, for instance, and I probably read more Dickens as a teenager than I have since as an adult. Contemporary humour attracted me (James Thurber and the American "witty" writers of the thirties), and I admired J.B. Priestly's novels, particularly *The Good Companions*. Australian writing seemed dull to me, no doubt because the rich pastures around my own back door then seemed so familiar.

I hope this is of some use to you.

Joan Lindsay

1896 – 1984

Joan, Lady Lindsay was born in St Kilda East, Victoria and educated at Carhue School which became Clyde School and later was re-located near to Mount Macedon. After graduating from Clyde, she decided to study art, enrolling at the National Gallery of Victoria Art School in 1916. There, while studying painting, she was taught by Bernard Hall and Frederick McCubbin. In 1920 she began sharing a Melbourne studio with Maie Ryan (later Lady Casey). Joan exhibited her watercolours and oils at two Melbourne exhibitions in 1920. She published her first literary work in 1936, a satirical novel titled "Through Darkest Pondelayo". Her second novel, "Time Without Clocks," was published nearly thirty years later, and was a semi-autobiographical account of the early years of her marriage to artist Sir Daryl Lindsay. In 1967, Lindsay published her most celebrated work, "Picnic at Hanging Rock", a novel detailing the vanishing of three schoolgirls and their teacher at the site of a monolith during one summer. The novel sparked critical and public interest for its ambivalent presentation as a true story as well as its vague conclusion, and is widely considered to be one of the most important Australian novels. It was adapted into a splendid film in 1975.

These were some of my favourite books as a teenager –

Round the World in Eighty Days – Jules Verne

Great Expectations – Charles Dickens

Alice's Adventures in Wonderland and *Through the Looking Glass* by Lewis Carroll

As there was no TV and no cinema until after I left school, I got from books some of the thrills and laughs that I get today from a favourite film. Your questionnaire asks if I was "influenced" by any of these books. Sorry, boys! I really don't know.

Jules Verne took me on a voyage round the world with an exciting glimpse of the unexplored future, which I can enjoy today by a trip to Outer Space at the cinema.

Great Expectations has such an intriguing plot and the people in it are so true to life that I often sat up late instead of doing my homework to see what happened in the next chapter.

Lewis Carroll, who wrote the 'Alice' books, was a surrealist before his time. They have the same sort of crazy slant as a Monty Python film with apparently ordinary people like ourselves doing the most un-ordinary things made miraculously real by a touch of genius.

I don't expect you to like all, or any, of my favourite books, because in reading matter 'one man's choice' is often 'another man's poison'. So why not take one out of the library that looks interesting; and if it bores you when you have read a couple of chapters, go back and take out another. Best wishes!

Archbishop Sir Frank Little

1925 – 2008

The Most Reverend Sir Frank Little, KBE, was born in Melbourne and educated at St Columba's School, Essendon, St Monica's College, Moonee Ponds, and St Patrick's College, Ballarat. He began training for the priesthood in 1943 at Corpus Christi College, Werribee, and later at Propaganda Fide College in Rome. He completed a doctorate at the Pontifical Urban University in Rome in 1953. Returning to Melbourne, he was appointed assistant priest to Carlton, then appointed assistant at St Patrick's Cathedral, Melbourne, in 1955. In 1965 he became the dean of the cathedral. He was appointed a Bishop in 1973 and Archbishop the following year and held office until 1996.

Congratulations on your initiative. I wish it every success.

You set my memory stirring as your interesting request came home to me.

P.C. Wren and John Buchan may well have come across my path, and thrilled me, prior to my becoming a teenager. I devoured the books of Maurice Walsh. My father regularly read to us: Shakespeare at times (giving us sufficient of selected readings to whet the appetite of my brothers and me); a short story of O'Henry often accompanied our Sunday dinner; Lawson, Paterson and O'Brien stirred deep feelings for my own country. As teenagers we must have heard from all of Conan Doyle's stories of Sherlock Holmes and Brigadier Gerard.

I can still recall the joy of discovery in relishing the prose descriptions of Dickens. Graham Greene and Evelyn Waugh (his *Edmund Campion* was my precious possession for many a year) were commencing to come into their own. Belloc and Chesterton were regular fare. P.G. Wodehouse sharpened my sense of humour with his delightful books. I felt I almost knew Mlton's *Paradise Lost* off by heart because I enjoyed it so much. The Penguin paperbacks made good books readily available.

The whole *Masterful Monk* series, written by Owen Francis Dudley, were attractive and appealing. T*he Life of Our Lord,* by Alban Goodier, brought home to me many fascinating aspects of Our Lord's life, while the English translations of the *New Testament* at this time left me distracted.

Alex Munthe in his *Story of San Michele* gave me a new understanding of human nature and a love of Capri. Alexis Carrell in *Man, the Unknown* also left me with a sense of inquiring wonder.

You know how it is. The very book with which I wanted to conclude this letter cannot be found; someone has thoughtfully tidied up my library. James Kelleher, the founder of the Christopher Movement, wrote what was for this teenager at that time a captivating book, *You Can Change the World.* His whole thesis was that purpose in life makes the difference. Whatever we do, we have a reason for doing it. The better the reason, the better the motive, then the better the deed, and more fulfilling for the person, the more inspiring life becomes. He proposed that people with purpose should enter employment with government, in education, and in those fields where they could influence others.

I have always been grateful for the fact that by reading that book I came to understand in a special way the power of ideas; I could see that ideas were changing me for the better, giving me vision, honing my ideals, enabling me to see personal maturity in service of others, challenging me to change the world.

Please excuse me. The requested few lines have become many.

Thank you for stimulating my own memories. "One day it will be realised that men are distinguishable from one another as much by the forms their memories take as by their characters" (Andre Malraux).

I take my leave, while retaining the anxious thought created by the inquiry of any school master: Did I answer the question?

With cordial greetings and every good wish.

John McCallum

1918 - 2010

John McCallum, AO, CBE, was born in Brisbane and educated at Harrogate School in England, at Brisbane Grammar School and the Royal Academy of Dramatic Art. In 1939, he returned to Australia to join the Second Australian Imperial Force for the duration of World War 2 and served in New Guinea. After a decade in England, he returned to Australia to be managing director of J.C. Williamson's, at that time the largest theatrical organization in the world, owning nine theatres, operating in 13 and mounting all its own productions, including "My Fair Lady" and "Camelot". In 1966 he went into film production, and produced or directed over 200 films for TV including the series "Skippy". In Australia he acted in many plays for J.C. Williamson's and in musical comedy. He was one of the greatest actors and directors of his generation, as well as a highly successful producer of theatre, film and television.

My apologies for this late reply to your letter of May 30th, but I've had a rather busy time these last few weeks putting on a play in Hobart.

To reply to the question:

In early teens I was all for adventure, particularly historical – hence Harrison Ainsworth (I read them all when I had my tonsils out, *The Tower of London* several times, Og, Gog & Magog, the three giants were my heroes for a long time), Rider Haggard (*She* made a big impact on puberty), Joseph Conrad of course, Sabatini (*Captain Blood* & tales about a woman pirate of the Spanish Main called Joanna).

Those ran concurrent with crime of course & Sexton Blake gave way to Edgar Wallace (*The Four Just Men* was my favourite) to G. Phillips Oppenheimer, an occasional Conan Doyle, Dorothy Sayers.

At about 14 I discovered Dickens – I had to, it was the set book for the year. A chore soon became a pleasure – the prescribed reading was *Pickwick Papers*, which soon had me laughing out loud. *Nicholas Nickleby* followed, & I think has to be my favourite, it was easy to identify with the horrible school & Squeers, & anyway I wanted to be a school teacher then, so Nicholas was my hero. I even liked *Little Dorrit*!

So *Nicholas Nickleby* with its story line, rich characters, pathos & comedy must be the answer as to which book has most influence.

Afterwards came Somerset Maugham, especially the short stories – I still re-read them – & before him were all the works of Jeffrey Farnol, Cecil Roberts (the romantic age!) And any plays I could get my hands on from J.M. Barrie to A.A. Milne – Shakespeare I found easier than Shaw! Only two Australian novels made an impression (at the time) *Robbery Under Arms, For the Term of his Natural Life*. Arthur Upfield and the Bonaparte books came later.

Hope this is not too late. What a good exercise – hope it stimulates interest in a few forgottens. Best wishes.

Alan McCulloch

1907 – 1992

Alan McCulloch, AO, was born in St Kilda and brought up in Mosman, Sydney. His father encouraged a sense that "the arts were the most important thing in life," so Alan developed keen interest in art as a child. The family returned to Melbourne after his father died. Alan was educated at Scotch College. He was employed in a clerical position at BHP in Melbourne, then worked as a teller with the Commonwealth Bank for eighteen years. Inspired in 1925 by hearing cartoonist Will Dyson speak on political satire and visiting his studio, he enrolled in night classes at RMIT and then the National Gallery School. He became art critic for "The Argus" in 1944. He travelled to America in 1947 and, on his return to Australia in 1951, he became art critic for "The Herald". His book, The Encyclopaedia of Australian Art was first published in 1968 and is still considered an outstanding reference work. He was one of Australia's foremost art critics for more than 60 years, an art historian and gallery director, cartoonist, and painter.

I read everything I could get my hands on, but the special readings I best remember were the Robert Louis Stevenson novels. I read them all, systematically, mostly in the train travelling to and from work. I'd left school at fifteen and was working in the city as an office boy, but fortunately I had access to a good library. I read all the novels, all the short stories, all the poems and all the letters. And if I came to words I didn't understand I'd write them in a little note book, look them up and memorise them.

I came out of it all with Stevenson's vocabulary. Stevenson's books led me to Voltaire, and Voltaire led me to the French novelists and so on . . . But Stevenson was my great love. He taught me about words. For example there was one word that virtually ruined *Treasure Island* for him. Referring to a diamond, he had written: "There it lay in the sand, winking up at me like a crumb of glass." Stevenson went on: "If only I hadn't used the word 'crumb'!"

Good reading.

F. Margaret McGuire

1900–1995

Frances Margaret McGuire, AM, was born on 20 May 1900 in Glenelg, South Australia. She attended the Girton House Girls' Grammar School and the University of Adelaide, where she studied life sciences. From 1923 to 1924, she worked in the laboratory which developed an improved method of delivering insulin. She was a co-founder of the Catholic Guild for Social Studies in Adelaide, South Australia in 1932, and served as the director of studies for the organization for sixteen years. She authored or co-authored more than ten books, including "Bright morning: The story of an Australian family before 1914", a handbook for Catholic Action *groups, and a history of the Royal Australian Navy.*

It is really too bad that I should have been so long replying to your letter of the 16th. But I have had builders all over the house and am living in a state of great confusion. So please accept my apologies.

How optimistic you must be if you think that your plan can improve the reading habits of your boys! It smacks (I must confess) to me too much of the modern habit of thinking that you can cure the ills of society by forming a committee and conducting a 'survey'. But, all the same, I admire you for trying. The other day a senior educationist was asked how he would encourage young people to read more. His answer was another question: 'Do you think books are so important? I think we can learn more by talking to people rather than by reading books!' So it cheers me up no end to know that at least one educationist thinks that his pupils should read.

About our own reading habits: My husband (who died in 1978) is of no use for this, because he was one of those omnivorous readers who by the time he was 20 had read the classics, most of English and French history, all the English poets, a mass of philosophy, the usual body of English belles-lettres, and so on. No science.

I, too, was a compulsive reader. I refer to my book *Bright Morning* which gives a pretty good run-down on my youthful reading. By the age of 15 I was reading natural history, at 16 Rudyard Kipling, masses of poetry, essays and biographies, popular science. From then to 20 more and more science, belles lettres and aesthetics. But this doesn't help you. I would say, let them read anything. In *Bright Morning* you will see that I read the brass plaques on the bath-heater. Also the boys comics (I loved *Puck*). Girls' papers lacked interest. Cowboys and Indians were popular, detective stories we both adored and have all the classics (Conan Doyle, Freeman, Christie, Sayers, Bentley, Chesterton, Rex Stout, etc. etc. – and Wilkie Collins and Dickens, of course). Then I found William de Morgan and the Russians; Jean Henri Fabre and J. Arthur Thomson, as well as H.G. Wells and Hilaire Belloc. This gets me to about 19 or 20 when of course I had to get into serious reading.

The only thing I can think of is to capture the mothers. We were always read aloud to, at night after getting into bed, during sewing lessons and drawing lessons at school. And the book would be passed around and everyone had to read a page or two, even if they red very badly.

In this way we worked through Jane Austen, the Brontes and a lot of Dickens. Some people liked Thomas Hardy and Walter Scott. I couldn't read them then, have made myself read them since, but would never return to them. But the boys loved *Ivanhoe*.

Our headmistress was a very keen English Lit. fan . . . She made every single girl in the school (of several hundreds of girls) write down a list of three or four books she would like to own if she won a prize. Sure enough, when the prizes were handed out at the end of the year, they included the titles of the girl's own choice. For the non-winners there was the useful exercise of thinking up what books they would like to have, and I suspect that their lists were handed on to parents looking for Christmas presents to buy.

Well, that's all I can think of. Encourage them to think of books like tuck-ins, meringues and cream puffs – in other words orgies. But to think vertically, because then the whole material universe is at your disposal. Think of *Dr Who* and the Greek, Cretan and Egyptian myths. And what s.f. owes to H.G. Wells and Jules Verne.

Books that influenced me:

The Forerunner by Merjkowski

The Day's Work by Kipling

La Vie de Pasteur by Vallery-Radot

The Poems of Robert Browning

All the works of John Ruskin and always, always, always the plays of Shakespeare and the *Book of the Prophet Isaiah*

And for heaven's sake don't be high-brow. If they read enough, taste, as in food, music, art and philosophy, will develop, and in the end they will only want the best. In the meantime, play the field. How marvellous to be at that age and have it all before you! Encourage them to wallow!

Sir William McKell

1891 - 1985

The Right Honourable Sir William McKell, GCMG, QC, served as the 12th Governor-General of Australia from 1947 to 1953. He had previously been Premier of New South Wales from 1941 to 1947, as leader of the Labour Party. He was born in Pambula, New South Wales, but grew up in Sydney. He left school at thirteen, training as a boilermaker. He soon became involved with the union movement, and after a brief period on the railways, began working full-time as a union secretary. He sided with the anti-conscriptionists during the Labour Party split of 1916 and, at the 1917 state election, defeated a former Labour premier who had been expelled from the party. In 1920, aged 29, he became Minister of Justice. He also served as a minister under the notorious Jack Lang.

Thank you for your letter seeking information about books that influenced me in my early years. To begin with, I must admit that the demands of my early occupation as a boilermaker and my later busy career in politics and law left me nothing like as much time as I could have desired to read and study. I have compiled, however, a short list of works that, although not the sort of thing that was read in polite society in those days, I recall as having had a strong impact on me as a young man.

The essays of Ralph Waldo Emerson

Plutarch's Lives

Thomas Moore's *Utopia*

Edward Bellamy's *Equality* and *Looking Backward*

Sidney and Beatrice Webb's *History of Trade Unionism* and *Industrial Democracy*

George Bernard Shaw's *Fabian Essays in Socialism*

Fabian Tracts

Winwood Reade's *Martyrdom of Man*

William Morris's *News from Nowhere*

Sir Charles Mackerras

1925 – 2010

Sir Charles Mackerras, AC, CH, CBE, was born in New York to Australian parents and came to Sydney at the age of two. He was a world-renowned conductor and authority on the works of Mozart, Janáček and the comic operas of Gilbert and Sullivan. Growing up in Sydney, he had a chequered schooling, attending Sydney Grammar School, St Aloysius College and then The King's School from which he was expelled. He studied at the Sydney Conservatorium and spent the following years working in Sydney, London and Prague with occasional returns to Australia. He was appointed conductor of the Sydney Symphony Orchestra in 1985. He directed the Welsh National Opera from 1987 to 1992 and was Principal Guest Conductor of the Royal Philharmonic Orchestra from 1993 to 1996. From 1999, he was Patron of the Australian children's cancer charity Redkite.

I always found European History, particularly the Eighteenth Century and the Nineteenth Century very absorbing, as presented in books such as Dickens' *Tale of Two Cities, David Copperfield* and Thackeray's *Vanity Fair*. I was also an avid reader of Sherlock Holmes and was fascinated by the milieu it depicted.

Ian McLaren

1912 – 2000

Ian McLaren, OBE was born at Launceston in Tasmania and educated at Caulfield Grammar School and the University of Melbourne. He served in the Royal Australian Navy from 1942 to 1945 and, after the war, he returned to Melbourne where he become a partner in the accountancy firm of Harris & McLaren. From 1945 to 1947 he was the independent member for Glen Iris in the Victorian Legislative Assembly. Following his defeat he joined the Liberal Party, and served on Malvern City Council from 1951 to 1953. In 1965, he returned to the Legislative Assembly as the Liberal member for Caulfield, changing seats to Bennettswood in 1967. From 1973, he was Deputy Speaker. McLaren retired from politics in 1979.

He was a long-standing member of the Royal Historical Society of Victoria and served as its President from 1956 to 1959. He was a prolific bibliographer and produced numerous published bibliographies, including major contributions to Australian bibliography. His first was "Local Histories of Australia" published in 1954. He was also a noted book collector and donated many books to the Baillieu Library at the University of Melbourne.

My apologies for this late reply to your letter of 16 September but we just returned over the weekend after several months abroad.

In answer to your question, I have been interested in books collectively for as long as I can remember. This led to the formation of "The McLaren Collection" now at the University of Melbourne comprising some 40,000 books and pamphlets on, or relating to, Australasia and the Pacific.

Here is a preliminary attempt to outline some of those influences and the books that have had the most important effects.

Parents. My parents believed that there should always be an adequate number of good reference books in the home. There was a set of *Historians' History of the World* as well as an old encyclopaedia and standard dictionary. My father was interested in the sea, travelling north or to New Zealand in his single days. We had books on the sea, all of which I read. This no doubt led me to join the RAN, and led to collecting naval and maritime books, especially shipwrecks. My mother was a music teacher and proud of her pre-war Ronisch on which I learned music; I also took elocution lessons for some years from Gwen Apted, during which I learned and recited large sections of verse and prose. My parents often took me through Cole's Book Arcade until it was closed in 1929; we seldom bought books because money was scarce, at the beginning of the depression. In later years as my own family went to school after World War II, I added many reference and literary books as I had become aware of their use in my own youth.

Spring Road Central School. I owe much to my year in 1925 with Miss Edith Hurrey at this school. Gardiner, Tooronga Road and Spring Road were three competitive scholarship centres. Miss Hurrey developed personal enquiry and wider reading of the classics. It was from here that I obtained my scholarship to Caulfield Grammar School.

Caulfield Grammar School 1926-9. Both F.H. Archer and Arthur Lormer still further opened up the classical literary world. We read Dickens, Scott, Thackeray, Dumas, Moliere, etc. I have little remembrance of the library at school, as books tended to be in the home, rather than in school and municipal libraries. Fiction libraries were usually run by little old ladies, with a lending rate of 3d per book.

Flack & Flack 1930-6. It was Arthur Lormer who introduced me to his brother George Lormer, a partner of Flack & Flack Chartered Accountants, later to become Price Waterhouse & Co. They had a strong technical library and insisted on their young staff studying and completing their accountancy, secretarial and costing examinations. One of their audits was Cassells, and I began acquiring their Classics series at 1/- per volume. Depression salaries were low and most of the income had to go into the family during those years. However there was seldom a week in which I did not buy a book. Encyclopaedia series, issued fortnightly, were also popular. My grandchildren still have some of the *World of Knowledge* series, which they now use for cutting, as did my own children. These series were a distinct educational aid.

Church. I read through the King James version of The Bible on several occasions. There could be few greater examples of literature than the Psalms. Once a month I attended the literary sermons of Dr F.W. Boreham at Armadale Baptist Church [see entry in Australian Dictionary of Biography 7/349] in which he used a book, from the classics to colloquial C.J. Dennis, to tell his story. This led me in turn to collect his considerable literary output. Secondly, my minister at Murrumbeena Presbyterian Church from 1926-1939 (?) was Rev. Aeneas MacDonald, author of *The history of the Presbyterian Church in Victoria*. MacDonald was not a good preacher and should have been an academic; he encouraged us to read and was generous in the loan of books from his extensive library, especially for debating.

Y.M.C.A. 1931-9. In the depression and pre-war years, I was involved in debating, lectures, meeting of authors. This led also to an interest in the Australian Youth Council, League of Nations Union and International Peace Campaign. As a foundation member of Rostrum No. 3 in Melbourne, I continued public speaking. The amount of preparation for a short speech means reading and reference of a high order if the speech is to be successful.

Argus and Australasian Ltd 1937-8. I had two years with this now defunct newspaper; here one met writers and authors, and became more interested in the written word.

Overseas Visit 1938-9. Australian youth organisations sent me abroad to attend five world youth conferences in USA, Canada, Uruguay and Holland. I found that much of my reading was useful for application to the wider world. It was most unusual for young people to travel abroad at that time because of the cost. The 18 months' tour cost me $600.

Apart from all the above, my favourite author as a teenager was no doubt Alexandre Dumas, all of whose books I read several times. They are well written and translated, with continuous action in a relatively uncomplicated period.

Sir William McMahon

1908 – 1988

The Right Honourable Sir William McMahon, GCMG, CH, PC, was born in Redfern and raised in Sydney and was educated at Sydney Grammar School and the University of Sydney. He served in the Australian Army during World War II, reaching the rank of major. After the war, he returned to university to complete an economics degree. He worked as a commercial lawyer before entering federal politics at the 1949 federal election. Robert Menzies promoted him to the ministry in 1951 and added him to cabinet in 1956. He held several different portfolios in the Menzies government, most notably as Minister for Labour and National Service from 1958 to 1966. He was a government minister for over 21 years, the longest continuous service in Australian history. He was Prime Minister of Australia from 1971 to 1972.

Referring to your letter of 16th September; after considerable thought, I felt it better to say that I am not a good example to answer your question on which books influenced me as a teenager and why.

I read what I had to, according to the class syllabus and concentrated almost exclusively on them, regrettably, in retrospect.

I started off being fascinated with ancient history, Latin and Greek. I do not think any of the books I read had any influence on my life.

Leonard Mann

1895 - 1981

Sadly, Leonard Mann is almost unknown today, although he was the author of one of the most significant novels of the Great War, "Flesh in Armour". He was unable to place it with a publisher in Australia or the UK so he published it privately in 1932. It was an immediate success and won the Australian Literature Society's Gold Medal for outstanding book of the year. It was reissued in 1944 but remained out of print until 2008 when it was published by the University of South Carolina Press and then by Penguin Australia in 2014. He had served in the AIF during the Great War and in the Ministry of Aircraft Production in World War II. He published six other novels and four volumes of poetry, winning the Grace Leven Prize for Poetry in 1957. In 1949, he became a charter member of the Australian Peace Council.

I have your letter of 10th July. I am, however, unable to make any precise answer to it – indeed any answer at all. Which doesn't mean that I did not read many books as a teenager. But I would find it quite impossible to distinguish now those which might be seen as favourites or as by degrees of influence. Your teacher can, I have no doubt, prepare lists of valuable, even great perhaps, works of fiction, in their original or in translations. I am too old to take part, being 85 years. Interesting how often crime is an activation.

Alan Marshall

1902 – 1984

Alan Marshall, AM, was born in Noorat, Victoria, and attended school in Terang. At six years of age, he contracted polio, which left him with a physical disability that grew worse as he grew older. From an early age, he resolved to be a writer, and in his best-known book, "I Can Jump Puddles", published in 1955, he demonstrated an almost total recall of his childhood in Noorat. It is the first of a three-part autobiography. The other two volumes are "This is the Grass" published in 1962 and "In Mine Own Heart" published the following year. During the early 1930s he worked as an accountant at the Trueform Boot and Shoe Company, Clifton Hill, and later wrote about life in the factory in his novel "How Beautiful are Thy Feet", published in 1949. He wrote numerous short stories, mainly set in the bush. He also wrote newspaper columns and magazine articles. He travelled widely in Australia and overseas. He also collected and published Indigenous Australian stories and legends.

I have had questions similar to those asked by you many times over the years and I have always wished that I could answer them truthfully with the statement that the books that influenced me most were Homer's *The Iliad*, The *Odyssey* or *Beowolf.* I thought being inspired by these wonderful epics would suggest that I myself had gained something from them

But it was not like that at all. One of the first books I can remember influencing my life was *The Swiss Family Robinson*! Then I read the books of Ballantyne, *The Gorilla Hunters* and books by

Edward S. Henty which glorified war and the British Empire.

But it was not until I first started Joseph Conrad that I became fanatical on all his work. I used to read his books slowly so that I could savour to the full the beauty of his prose. He wrote one long short story called *Heart of Darkness* which made me realize what great literature really meant. Then I read *The Nigger of the Narcissus, Lord Jim* and *The Mirror of the Sea.* Conrad's books gripped me. They gave me an idea of the power a good writer has to evoke an experience.

I then began to read Maxim Gorky and read the three volumes of his autobiography which gave me a wonderful picture of his grandmother and of how he had suffered at school.

Now that I am old I find the greatest pleasure in reading *The Crock of Gold* by James Stephens. I have now read *The Iliad* and *The Odyssey* a number of times and am on my third reading of *Beowolf.*

So, really, I now find that great literature springs from the people. It is the epic folk tales that I love – the tales that tell of fabulous heroes . . . Of men who conquered evil in the shape of a dragon until ultimately good prevailed.

Being old brings with it a need to be optimistic about the future and life generally. These tales may be escape tales, but so is television and I would sooner read *The Iliad* than look at *The Sullivans.*

So don't forget – read The *Crock of Gold* as soon as you get a chance. It is full of wisdom and that's what we want today.

Bert Newton

1938 – 2021

Bert Newton, AM, MBE, was an Australian media personality. He was born in Fitzroy and educated at St Joseph's College. His first paid radio appearance was as a schoolboy on Melbourne radio station 3XY. In May 1954, 3XY employed him as a junior announcer (aged 15); by 1955, he was presenting "Melbourne Speaks", a vox pop *program recorded on the streets of Melbourne's CBD. He became a star and fixture of Australian television from its inception in 1956, and was considered both an industry pioneer icon and one of the longest-serving television performers in the world. He was known for his collaborations opposite Graham Kennedy and subsequently Don Lane on their respective variety shows, and appearances with his wife, singer Patti Newton. He was a Logie Hall of Fame inductee and quadruple Gold Logie winner.*

Three books stand out from my childhood years and each of them still holds pride of place in my Library, probably as much for sentimental reasons as for any other.

The Water Babies by Charles Kingsley has a special place in my memory because it is the first book I can recall studying at school and it was my first real introduction to the joy of reading.

In my early teenage years *Tom Sawyer* by Mark Twain was close to everybody's favourite and I was no exception.

In my later teenage years *Elected Silence* by Thomas Merton presented a huge challenge. I could not fully understand it then and many years later it still required close reading and careful digestion.

These three stand out in a sea of childhood literary memories.

Gerald O'Collins

Born 1931

World-renowned theologian the Reverend Gerald O'Collins, SJ, AC, was born in Melbourne and educated at Xavier College and the University of Melbourne where he graduated with a Master of Arts degree. Then followed a Licentiate of Sacred Theology from London University, Doctor of Philosophy from the University of Cambridge and a Doctor of Divinity from the University of Melbourne. He has been Professor of Theology at universities in the UK, USA and was Dean of Theology at the Gregorian University in Rome from 1985 to 1991. He is now based at the Jesuit Theological College in Melbourne. He is the author, co-author or editor of over 70 books.

I am sorry you have had to wait a bit for a reply, but your letter reached me just as I was leaving Rome for New York and then San Francisco (where I am teaching a summer programme). Alas, I can't make it back to Melbourne this year.

As a teenager I found Shakespeare's great plays, especially *Macbeth* and *Hamlet* my favourites. He expresses in such strong and luminous language very many basic human convictions and reflections about loyalty, time, guilt, the meaning of existence, love, the threat of death and the rest.

Andrew Peacock

1939 – 2021

The Honourable Andrew Peacock, AC, was born in Melbourne and attended Elsternwick Primary School and Scotch College before studying law at the University of Melbourne. He was elected to Parliament at the age of 27, for the seat of Kooyong, vacated by Sir Robert Menzies. He was appointed to cabinet in 1969. He held a variety of portfolios, most notably serving as Minister for Foreign Affairs from 1975 to 1980. He unsuccessfully challenged Malcolm Fraser for the Liberal leadership in 1982, but was then elected as Fraser's successor following the party's defeat at the 1983 election. Peacock left politics in 1994 and was later appointed Ambassador to the United States, serving from 1997 to 1999.

I refer to your letter of 30 May and would have to advise that it was books I read in the latter stage of my teens that were of more influence than the earlier stage. Sargeant's *Battle in the Mind,* Sir Frederic Eggleston 's *Reflections of an Australian Liberal,* Barbara Ward's *Faith and Freedom* and Alfred Deakin's *The Federal Story,* are four that come to mind. Doubtless, there are many others.

For example, Theodore White's account of the Presidential elections on 1960 and the later biographies of John Kennedy were of enormous influence on me, but of course, read in my early twenties. Apart from that, many of the required reading texts, particularly in the field of history, were of importance to me. As I learnt at a very early period in my life, that albeit societies change, people react under pressure in many similar ways and therefore most required history texts were of a considerable influence in the formation of my political philosophy.

Stuart Sayers

1923 – 1993

Born in Melbourne and educated at Ivanhoe Grammar School and Geelong Grammar School, Stuart Sayers served in the Royal Australian Navy in World War 2 in the waters north of Australia and surrounding New Guinea and in the Pacific. He spent three years in London with Australian Associated Press and Reuter before returning to Australia. In 1964, he became Literary Editor of "The Age". His books include "The Company of Books: A Short History of the Lothian Book Companies, 1888 – 1988", "Ned Herring: A life of Lieutenant General the Honourable Sir Edmund Herring" and "By courage and faith: The first fifty years of Carey Baptist Grammar School".

I have been giving some thought to your letter of 24 June and at somewhat of a loss to reply. I simply cannot remember clearly what I was reading as a teenager. I hate to confess how long ago that was.

My first difficulty is that I am not too sure which are the teenage years. But I seem to remember that I had an especially precocious spell of devouring Dickens at the age of ten or eleven. *David Copperfield, Oliver Twist, Barnaby Rudge, The Old Curiosity Shop* and *The Tale of Two Cities* stick in my mind most firmly.

I then lapsed into a regrettable infatuation with *Tarzan of the Apes,* and, even more reprehensible, *Beau Geste.*

For some reason I cannot explain how *Sons and Lovers* lingers in my memory as a book which greatly impressed me at about the age of fifteen. I don't think I liked it much but it did overwhelm me. Of course I was also reading many ephemeral things, such as the *Magnet* and the *Gem* and, I suppose, newspapers. But it is difficult at this distance to recall precisely all or any books I read between the ages of, say, nine and sixteen.

I am no longer sure when I read Jane Austen or Dumas, for instance, but they both fill an important place in the fabric of my literary nourishment as a boy. So, too, do Stevenson, R.M. Ballantyne, Kipling and, of the Australians, Mary Grant Bruce, which is I suppose a revealing confession. I doubt if I could read any of them now.

Is this of any use? I have been surprised and rather disconcerted to discover how little I can remember of what I did read so long ago – except of course Tarzan and the boys' comics of those times, all of them British.

Sir Billy Snedden

1926 - 1987

The Honourable Sir Billy Snedden, KCMG, QC, was born in Perth and educated at Highgate State School and Perth Boys' High School but left in 1942 to work as a law clerk. In 1944, he joined the Commonwealth Crown Solicitor's Office. The next year, he enlisted in the RAAF and trained as an aircraftman at Busselton in Western Australia, and Somers in Victoria, before being discharged on 14 September as the war had ended. Eligible to further his education under the Commonwealth Reconstruction Training Scheme, he entered the law faculty at the University of Western Australia and graduated in 1950. He was elected as a member of the federal parliament in 1955. A QC from Melbourne, he held the post of Attorney General in the Menzies government from 1964 to 1967. He was federal Treasurer in 1971 and 1972, before replacing Billy McMahon as leader of the Liberal Party. In 1974 he narrowly lost the election to Gough Whitlam. The following year he was replaced as leader by Malcolm Fraser. He remained Speaker of House of Representatives from 1976 to 1983.

The project your students have devised sounds interesting and worthwhile. Its results should receive a wider circulation.

Because I worked throughout my "teens", including while I was at school, I had very little time for my own reading. When I did read it was mainly curricular.

One book that I carry with me still is a text book from when I studied Logic. The book discussed different ways of thinking and it points out faults that people very often develop. I have always found it helpful. It's a very good book to sharpen up your own thinking and to keep it sharp. It is called *Traditional Formal Logic.*

I have always spent a lot of time keeping in touch with current affairs. This often involves a great deal of reading, but mainly of a current issues nature.

I have always regretted the lack of time available for optional reading in my area of work – all politicians and politics in general suffer by it. I can only suggest to you who are lucky enough to have it that you use your reading time.

Peter Sculthorpe

1929 – 2014

Peter Sculthorpe, AO, OBE, was born in Tasmania and educated at Launceston Grammar School. He began writing music at the age of seven or eight. By 14, he had decided to make a career of music because he felt the music he wrote was the only thing that was his own. He studied at the Melbourne Conservatorium of Music from 1946 to 1950, then returned to Tasmania. He was awarded a scholarship to study at the University of Oxford. Much of his music resulted from an interest in the music of countries neighbouring Australia as well as from the impulse to bring together aspects of Aboriginal music with that of the heritage of the West. In 1963 he became a lecturer at the University of Sydney, and remained there more or less ever after, In 1965 he wrote "Sun Music I" for the Sydney Symphony Orchestra's first overseas tour, on a commission from Sir Bernard Heinze, He was known primarily for his orchestral and chamber music, such as "Kakadu" and "Earth Cry", which evoke the sounds and feeling of the Australian bushland and outback. He also wrote 18 string quartets, using unusual timbral effects, works for piano, and two operas.

I do apologise for this late reply to your letter: I've been writing a guitar concerto for John Williams, and my correspondence as been somewhat neglected. I give below my answers to your questions.

I was very fortunate as a young boy, because my mother, having been a teacher, encouraged me to read, and guided my choice of books. Thus, before I reached my 'teens I had read most of the great works written in the English language. I was also fortunate in that television did not exist at that time, and so most of my leisure was spent in reading. During my 'teens I did less reading, apart from French and English poetry; I had decided that I would become a composer, and therefore I devoted all my spare time to writing music.

My ten favourite books, or those that influenced me most, that changed my life in some way, are, in random order:

James Joyce: *Portrait of the Artist as a Young Man*

Joseph Conrad: *Lord Jim*

A.A. Milne: *Winnie the Pooh*

John Drinkwater (ed): *The Outline of Literature*

T.S. Eliot: *Prufrock & Other Observations*

Thomas Malory: *The Death of King Arthur*

Herman Melville: *Typee*

D.H. Lawrence: *Kangaroo*

Concise History of the World (Illustrated) published by Universal Books, London, 1935.

Friedrich Nietzche: *Thus Spake Zarathustra*

I have enjoyed thinking about your project; somehow, in making up the above list I learned a great deal about myself. I imagine that the above books influenced me because they provided me with some kind of identification, &, in several cases, some kind of revelation.

My best wishes to you and the boys in Year 11 English.

Dame Joan Sutherland

1926 – 2010

Dame Joan Sutherland, OM, AC, DBE, was born in Sydney to Scottish parents and attended St Catherine's School. In 1951, she made her stage debut in Eugene Goossens's "Judith". She then went to London to further her studies at the Opera School of the Royal College of Music. She was then engaged by the Royal Opera House, Covent Garden. She sang Lucia to great acclaim in Paris in 1960 and, in 1961, at La Scala and the Metropolitan Opera. In 1960 she sang Alcina at La Fenice in Venice. Sutherland would soon be praised as "La Stupenda" in newspapers around the world. She possessed a voice combining agility, accurate intonation, pinpoint staccatos, a trill and a strong upper register.

To answer your question: As a teenager, I remember most enjoying the novels of Jane Austen and books about European Travel and History. I think we are tremendously fortunate nowadays to have so many wonderfully written and illustrated books to read. One only wishes there was more time to read them all.

Colin Thiele

1920 – 2006

Colin Thiele, AC, was born in Eudunda, South Australia. He was educated at several country schools including the Eudunda Higher Primary School, and Kapunda High School before studying at the University of Adelaide, graduating in 1941. He enlisted in the Australian Army in December 1940, and was posted to the 18th Light Horse (Machine Gun) as a private. He transferred to the Royal Australian Air Force in July 1942, serving out the remainder of the war as a corporal posted to Air Defence Headquarters at the tip of the Cape York Peninsula. He later taught in high schools and colleges. He became principal of Wattle Park Teachers College in 1965, principal of Murray Park CAE in 1973, and director of the Wattle Park Teachers Centre until his retirement in 1980. He was renowned for his award-winning children's fiction, most notably the novels "Storm Boy", "Blue Fin", the "Sun on the Stubble" series, and "February Dragon".

Thank you for your letter of 30 May describing your Year 11 English project.

It is a little difficult to look back forty or fifty years and to state with complete certainty that I did this or that at a particular time. However I do remember some of the books of my boyhood very vividly indeed.

The first thing I should stress is that when I was a small boy very few books were available for us to read. The "library" in the little bush school I went to consisted of a shelf with twenty or thirty books on it, and my mother had a few German novels at home. I read all of these avidly because there were no such things as T.V., radio, cinema, taped music, record players or other forms of mass entertainment. We also read the *Bible* in both German and English.

I would divide the books I read at that time into four main groups:

1. Adventure stories
   These were yarns about shipwrecks, desert islands, pirates, Red Indians, and jungle exploration. Three stand out above the rest – *The Swiss Family Robinson, Treasure Island* and *Robinson Crusoe*.
2. English schoolboy stories
   On the whole these were dreadful books about boarding school life and rugby matches which I didn't even understand.
3. Australian books
   When I was about 12 I went to secondary school and was able to read some of the pioneer Australian books such as *Robbery Under Arms, On Our Selection, For the Term of his Natural Life, Paving the Way* and *Seven Little Australians*. But of all these I thought *While the Billy Boils* by Henry Lawson was the most remarkable in its ability to turn characters into real flesh-and-blood people. The boy milking the cow in one of the sketches was so real that he could have been me.
4. Important Novels by English Writers
   Between the ages of 14 and 16 I read large numbers of so-called "classics" – much of Dickens, Thomas Hardy, Joseph Conrad and so on. At the age of 16 I enrolled at the University where I read vast numbers of books – poetry and prose by most of the great English and American writers, and translations of French and Russian poets and novelists.

To answer your question is therefore very difficult. It depends on the definition of "teenager". If I restrict this to my early teens (say, to 15) I guess the Australian writers – especially Lawson – influenced me most because I understood the spirit of the people and the land he was writing about.

Lindsay Thompson

1923 – 2008

The Honourable Lindsay Thompson, AO, CMG, was born in Warburton. He attended Caulfield Grammar School where he was School Captain and Dux of School. He served in the Australian Army in New Guinea during World War II then graduated from the University of Melbourne. Elected to the Victorian Parliament in 1955, he served a record term as a minister from 1958 to 1982. He was Premier of Victoria from June 1981 to April 1982. His autobiography, "I Remember", was published in 1989.

I do recall three books in particular which I read in my Leaving Certificate year. They were *Barlasch of the Guard*, *The Crisis* by Winston Churchill and a book entitled *From Log Cabin to White House*. The latter was a biography of the life of James Garfield, one of the United States Presidents who was assassinated.

The last-mentioned book I recall reading several times. It had great appeal to me at that age. *The Crisis* was also a fascinating book based on the struggle between North and South in the American Civil War. It provided an excellent insight into and understanding of the colour problem which still tends to divide the U.S.A.

Archbishop Sir Frank Woods

1907 – 1992

The Most Reverend Sir Frank Woods, KBE, was born in 1907 in Davos, Switzerland. In 1914, the family moved to England where Frank was educated at Marlborough College and Cambridge University. He was ordained as a priest in 1932. After a curacy at St Mary's Church, Portsea in the Diocese of Portsmouth he became chaplain of Trinity College, Cambridge. He then became Vice-Principal of Wells Theological College. During the Second World War, he served as a chaplain in the Royal Naval Volunteer Reserve and then, successively, a vicar in Huddersfield from 1945 to 1952, Suffragan Bishop of Middleton from 1952 to 1957 and, in 1957, Archbishop of Melbourne for over 20 years. From 1971 he was also the Anglican Primate of Australia.

Your class will think me very dull when I reply to your letter for I find it almost impossible to think of books that influenced me in my 'teens'. I don't think that at that age books did influence me much. I read a fair deal but it was for enjoyment and even here it isn't individual books that I remember now, but authors. I think – but couldn't swear to it – that I enjoyed a lot of Dickens, especially *Dombey and Son*, a fair deal of Rider Haggard but I can't remember the titles; the stories of the author of *The Thirty-nine Steps* (can't think of his name: he became Governor-General of Canada),* and Kipling's *Kim*. We used to read out loud on summer holidays (we were all at boarding schools). I remember my father reading several of the historical novels of the American Winston Churchill. I think it was at that time of my life that I began to appreciate Hardy.

I think it may be true that Dickens did influence me by his revelation of the terrible squalor of London's poor and made me hope that one day I might do something about the underprivileged. My father used to read Dickens's *A Christmas Carol* out loud to us every Christmas.

*[The author of *The Thirty-nine Steps* was John Buchan]

Sir John Young

1919 – 2008

The Honourable Sir John Young, AC, KCMG, KStJ, QC, was Chief Justice of the Supreme Court of Victoria from 1974 to 1991. He was educated at Geelong Grammar School before studying at Brasenose College, Oxford, graduating with a Master of Arts degree. He served with distinction as an officer in the Scots Guards during World War II. On returning to Australia, he completed a Law degree at the University of Melbourne. A brilliant commercial lawyer, he was admitted to the Victorian Bar in 1949. As Chief Justice, he was recognized as a fine administrator and reformer.

I have found it difficult to recall the books which were my favourites when I was in my teens and even more difficult to remember the books which influenced me in those days. I suspect that those which I enjoyed most influenced me most.

I do, however, remember well reading John Galsworthy and Charles Morgan. The last of the Galsworthy trilogies, *Over the River* was published, I think, in about 1934, and after reading that I set out to read *The Forsyte Saga*, *The Modern Comedy* and *The End of the Chapter*. *The Forsyte Saga* was written before the television series! Galsworthy seemed to me to bring to life the immediate past and the times just before one's own hold a great deal of fascination for most people.

I also read Charles Morgan to whose College in Oxford I went at the end of my teens. He was, of course, a deeper thinker than John Galsworthy and I have no doubt that *The Flashing Stream* and particularly the introductory essay of singleness of mind or singleness of purpose or something of the sort influenced me considerably at the time.

I developed early an interest in language and one of the anthologies that I most enjoyed was *Pages of English Prose* by Sir Arthur Quiller-Couch. I rather think that it has been expanded and re-issued under the title *The Oxford Book of English Prose*. I cannot lay my hands on my copy but if I remember correctly it contained some very fine pieces of prose writing. One that comes to mind is Walter Pater's piece on the Mona Lisa, a very fine piece of writing. Incidentally Walter Pater was another Brasenose man, not as an under-graduate, but as a Fellow, but I never read as much of him subsequently as I should have.

Bibliography of the books cited

A Christmas Carol by Charles Dickens

A Connecticut Yankee in King Arthur's Court by Mark Twain

A Dash to Khartoum by G.A. Henty

A Doll's House by Henrik Ibsen

A History of Architecture by Sir Banister Fletcher

Alice's Adventures in Wonderland by Lewis Carroll

All Quiet on the Western Front by Erich Maria Remarque

A *Modern Comedy* by John Galsworthy

A l'Ouest rien de nouveau by Henri Remarque

Anna Karenina by Leo Tolstoy

Arms and the Man by George Bernard Shaw

Around the World in 80 Days by Jules Verne

A Selection of the War Letters, Prayers and Spiritual Writings of Fr Willie Doyle

Atlas Shrugged *by Ayn Rand*

Australian Insects by Walter Wilson Froggatt

Barlasch of the Guard by Hugh Stowell Scott

Barnaby Rudge by Charles Dickens

Barrack Room Ballads by Rudyard Kipling

Battle for the Mind by William Sargent

Beowulf

Berry & Co. by Dornford Yates

Beau Geste by P.C. Wren

Belinda of the Red Cross by Robert W. Hamilton

Birds of the Port Phillip District of New South Wales by John Collon

Brave New World by Aldous Huxley

Bright Morning by F. Margaret McGuire

Candide by Voltaire

Captain Blood: His Odyssey by Rafael Sabatini

Captain Desmond, VC by Maud Diver

Captains Courageous by Rudyard Kipling

Castle Gay by John Buchan

Catriona by Robert Louis Stevenson

Chang by Elizabeth Morse

Clarence Darrow for the Defence by Julius Stone

Commando by Denys Reitz

Concise History of the World Illustrated by Sir John Marriott

Coral Island by R.M. Ballantyne

Crime and Punishment by Fyodor Dostoevsky

Darkness at Noon by Arthur Koestler

David Copperfield by Charles Dickens

Death in Venice by Thomas Mann

Decline and Fall of the Roman Empire by Edward Gibbon

Destiny Bay by Donn Byrne

Devil Water by Anya Seton

Dombey and Son by Charles Dickens

Droll Stories by Honoré de Balzac

Dusty by Frank Dalby Davison

Elected Silence by Thomas Merton

End of the Chapter by John Galsworthy

Endurance: Shackleton's Incredible Journey by Alfred Lansing

Engineering Today by Thomas W. Corbin

England Have My Bones by T.H. White

Equality and Looking Backward by Edward Bellamy

Eric or Little by Little by Frederic Farrar

Escape of the Notorious Sir William Means by William Gosse Hay

Essays of Ralph Waldo Emerson

Everybody's Political What's What by George Bernard Shaw

Fabian Essays in Socialism by George Bernard Shaw

Faith and Freedom by BarbaraWard

Father and Son by Edmund Gosse

For The Term of His Natural Life by Marcus Clarke

For the White Cockade by Admiral Lord Mountevans

Fountainhead by Ayn Rand

From Log Cabin to White House by William Makepeace Thayer

Gargantua and Pantagruel by Rabelais

Gone With the Wind by Margaret Mitchell

Great Expectations by Charles Dickens

Greenmantle by John Buchan

Gulliver's Travels by Jonathan Swift

Hamlet by William Shakespeare

Heart of Darkness by Joseph Conrad

Her Privates We by Frederic Manning

Here's Luck by Lennie Lower

Hereward the Wake by Charles Kingsley

History of the English Speaking Peoples by Sir Winston Churchill

Huckleberry Finn by Mark Twain

Huntingtower by John Buchan

Hymns Ancient and Modern

I Can Jump Puddles by Alan Marshall

Ivanhoe by Sir Walter Scott

It Can't Happen Here by Sinclair Lewis

Jude the Obscure by Thomas Hardy

Julius Caesar by William Shakespeare

Jungle Stories by Rudyard Kipling

Just So Stories by Rudyard Kipling

Justice by John Galsworthy

Kangaroo by D.H. Lawrence

Kidnapped by Robert Louis Stevenson

Kim by Rudyard Kipling

King John by William Shakespeare

King Lear by William Shakespeare

King Solomon's Mines by H. Rider Haggard

Kipps by H.G. Wells

La vie de Pasteur by René Vallery-Radot

Le Morte d'Arthur by Thomas Mallory

Les Misérables by Victor Hugo

Letters From Iceland by W.H. Auden and Louis MacNeice

Letters to Young Churches by J.B. Phillips

Life of Edward Marshall Hall by Edward Marjoribanks

Little Dorrit by Charles Dickens

Lives of the Hunted by Ernest Thompson Seton

Lord Jim by Joseph Conrad

Lord of the Flies by William Golding

Lorna Doone by R.D. Blackmore

Love and Mr Lewisham by H.G. Wells

Love's Labour's Lost by William Shakespeare

Loyalties by John Galsworthy

Main Street by Sinclair Lewis

Man, the Unknown by Alexis Carrell

Martyrdom of Man by William Winwood Reade

Masterful Monk by Owen Francis Dudley

Melmoth the Wanderer by Charles Maturin

Memoirs of a Dutiful Daughter by Simone de Beauvoir

Memoirs of an Infantry Officer by Siegfried Sassoon

Montrose by John Buchan

Mr Midshipman Easy by Frederick Marryat

My Brilliant Career by Miles Franklin

Myths and Legends of Ancient Greece and Rome by E.M. Berens

News from Nowhere by William Morris

Nicholas Nickleby by Charles Dickens

Northwest Passage by Kenneth Roberts

Oliver Twist by Charles Dickens

One Hundred Years of Presbyterianism in Victoria by Aeneas MacDonald

On Our Selection by Steele Rudd

Our Mutual Friend by Charles Dickens

Over the River *by John Galsworthy*

Paving the Way by Simpson Newland

Philosophic Dictionary by Voltaire

Pickwick Papers by Charles Dickens

Poems of Henry Lawson

Poems of Banjo Paterson

Portrait of the Artist as a Young Man by James Joyce

Pride and Prejudice by Jane Austen

Progress and Poverty by Henry George

Prologue for the Canterbury Tales by Geoffrey Chaucer

Puck of Pook's Hill by Rudyard Kipling

Quentin Durward by Sir Walter Scott

Reach For the Sky by Paul Brickhill

Redgauntlet by Sir Walter Scott

Redheap by Norman Lindsay

Reflections of an Australian Liberal by Sir Frederick Eggleston

Rewards and Fairies by Rudyard Kipling

Ring of Bright Water by Gavin Maxwell

Robbery Under Arms by Rolf Boldrewood

Robinson Crusoe by Robert Louis Stevenson

Rogue Herries by Hugh Walpole

Round the Horn Before the Mast by Bssil Lubbock

Sanders of the River by Edgar Wallace

Saturdee by Norman Lindsay

Selected Verse by John Manifold

Seven Little Australians by Ethel Turner

Seven Pillars of Wisdom by T.E. Lawrence

Shakespearean Tragedy by A.C. Bradley

She by H. Rider Haggard

Short Stories by Henry Lawson

Silas Marner by George Eliot

Songs of a Campaign by Leon Gellert

Sons and Lovers by D.H. Lawrence

Stalky & Co. by Rudyard Kipling

Strife by John Galsworthy

Such is Life by Joseph Furphy

Survive the Savage Sea by Douglas Robertson

Swallows and Amazons by Arthur Ransome

Tale of Two Cities by Charles Dickens

Tales from the Hills by Rudyard Kipling

Tarzan of the Apes by Edgar Rice Burropughs

Tell England by Jack London

Tess of the d'Urbervilles by Thomas Hardy

The Aeneid by Virgil

The Apology of Socrates by Plato

The Bible

T*he Black Riders* by Amy Violet Needham

The Book of Common Prayer

The Call of the Wild by Jack London

The Catcher in the Rye by J.D. Salinger

The Celebrity by Winston Churchill

The Children's Treasure House by Arthur Mee (ed)

The Cloister and the Hearth by Charles Reade

The Club of Queer Trades by G.K. Chesterton

The Count of Monte Cristo by Alexandre Dumas

The Crisis by Winston Churchill

The Crock of Gold by James Stephens

The Crossing by Winston Churchill

The Daughters of Ishmael series by Diane Stringam Tolley

The Day's Work by Rudyard Kipling

The Deerslayer by Fenimore Cooper

The Diary of Willie Doyle

The Doctor's Dilemma by George Bernard Shaw

The Federal Story by Alfred Deakin

The Flashing Stream by Charles Morgan

The Flight of the Heron by D.K. Broster

The Forerunner by Dmitri Merezhkovsky

The Forsyte Saga by John Galsworthy

The Fortunes of Richard Mahoney by Henry Handel Richardson

The Foundation and Empire by Isaac Asimov

The Four Just Men by Edgar Wallace

The Golden Treasury by Francis Turner Palgrave

The Good Companions by J.B. Priestly

The Grapes of Wrath by John Steinbeck

The Hill: A Romance of Friendship by Horace Annesley Vachell

The Home of Mankind by Hendrik van Loon

The History of Mr Polly by H.G. Wells

The Hound of the Baskervilles by Sir Arthur Conan Doyle

The House at Pooh Corner by A.A. Milne

The Iliad by Homer

The Last Days of Pompeii by Lord Bulwer Lytton

The Last Enemy by Richard Hillary

The Last of the Mohicans by Fenimore Cooper

The Laughing Man by Victor Hugo

The Liberation of Mankind by Hendrik van Loon

The Life and Opinions of Tristram Shandy, Gentleman by Laurence Sterne

The Life of Our Land by Alban Goodier

The Magic Pudding by Norman Lindsay

The Man in the Iron Mask by Alexandre Dumas

The Master of Ballantrae by Robert Louis Stevenson

The Mayor of Casterbridge by Thomas Hardy

The Merchant of Venice by William Shakespeare

The Mirror of the Sea by Joseph Conrad

The Moon and Sixpence by W. Somerset Maugham

The Nigger of the Narcissus by Joseph Conrad

The Odyssey by Homer

The Old Curiosity Shop by Charles Dickens

The Outline of Literature by John Drinkwater (ed)

The Oxford Book of English Prose by Sir Arthur Quiller-Couch (ed)

The Oxford Book of Modern Verse by W.B. Yeats (ed)

The Perfect Tribute by Mary Raymond Shipman Andrews

The Physiography of Victoria by E. Sherbon Hills

The Poems of Adam Lindsay Gordon

The Poems of John Keats

The Poems of John Milton

The Poems of Robert Browning

The Prelude by William Wordsworth

The Recollections of Geoffrey Hamlyn by Henry Kingsley

The Red and the Black by Stendahl

The Research Magnificent by H.G. Wells

The Return of the Native by Thomas Hardy

The Roman and the Teuton by Charles Kingsley

The Scarlet Pimpernel by Baroness Orczy

The Sleeper Awakes by H.G. Wells

The Speckled Band by Sir Arthur Conan Doyle

The Story of Mankind by Hendrik van Loon

The Story of San Michele by Axel Munthe

The Swiss Family Robinson by Johann David Wyss

The Sword in the Stone by T.H. White

The Tempest by William Shakespeare

The Thin Blue Line by Charles Graves

The Thirty-nine Steps by John Buchan

The Three Musketeers by Alexandre Dumas

The Traditional Formal Logic by William Angus Sinclair

The Travels and Surprising Adventures of Baron Munchausen by Rudolf Erich Raspe

The Undying Fire by H.G. Wells

The War in the Air by H.G. Wells

The War of the Worlds by H.G. Wells

The Water Babies by Charles Kingsley

The White Company by Sir Arthur Conan Doyle

The Wind in the Willows by Kenneth Grahame

The *William* books by Richmal Compton

Theatre Street by Tamara Kasavina

There's No Such Thing as a Free Lunch by Milton Friedman

Three Lives by Gertrude Stein

Through the Looking Glass by Lewis Carroll

Thus Spake Zarathustra by Freiedrich Netzche

Tom Brown's Schooldays by Thomas Hughes

The History of Tom Jones, a Foundling by Henry Fielding

Tom Sawyer by Mark Twain

Treasure Island by Robert Louis Stevenson

Twelfth Night by William Shakespeare

Twinkletoes by Thomas Burke

Typee by Herman Melville

Ulysses by James Joyce

Under the Red Robe by Stanley Weyman

Utopia by Thomas More

Vanity Fair by William Makepeace Thackeray

Vathek by William Beckford

Verse Worth Remembering by Stanley Maxwell

War and Peace by Leo Tolstoy

Westward Ho! by Charles Kingsley

Wild Animals I have Known by Ernest Thompson Seton

Winnie the Pooh by A.A. Milne

White Fang by Jack London

Wulf the Saxon by G.A. Henty

Wuthering Heights by Emily Bronte

War and Peace by Leo Tolstoy

Westward Ho! by Charles Kingsley

We the Living by Ayn Rand

White Fang by Jack London

Wild Animals I have Known by Ernest Thompson Seton

Winnie the Pooh by A.A. Milne

Wulf the Saxon by G.A. Henty

Wuthering Heights by Emily Bronte

You Can Change the World by James Kelleher

Acknowledgements

I begin by thanking the students of my Year 11 English class. They must have wondered what on earth they had struck when this new English master suggested that they write several hundred letters to people all over Australia. They soon took up the idea and we had a great deal of fun, particularly when the replies started coming back. Each morning's post became something we looked forward to with real anticipation.

Thanks are also due to Professor Simon Smith, who encouraged me to put the letters into a book; to Stan Kurrle and Bill Callander, who showed me what good teachers do; and to those students who, over more than 40 years, made me realise, with absolute certainty, that I could not have made a better choice than to be a teacher.

David Thomson

November, 2023

Milton Keynes UK
Ingram Content Group UK Ltd.
UKHW022042290324
440241UK00015B/656